Remington

BOOK 1 OF THE LADIES OF
THE BLUE MOON SALOON
SERIES

JAMIE SPICER

Acknowledgements:

Mom: I love you, thank you for birthing me.

Courtney: Thanks for your continued support of my writing. I love you.

Samantha: Thanks for always cheering me on. I don't know if I would still be up to putting books out there if it weren't for you. I appreciate you more than you know.

Cassandra: Thanks for everything. You are awesome.

Jacob (@thebeardedbullguy) I appreciate you answering my questions and letting me be a pain in your neck. I hope nothing but the best for you in your future,

Alexis (@thatbullgirl) Thank you for answering my questions and putting on a hell of a show!

Andrea: Thank you for being my cover model and giving Remington a face. I appreciate it.

Jenn: Thanks for helping me. You are amazing.

Dear Reader,

Thank you to the people who bought Curveball and Screwball and took a chance on me. I truly appreciate the re-postings, the congratulations, and the good jobs that I got. I don't have many supporters around me, but I am so happy that I have made friends throughout the reading and writing community who want to see new authors succeed.

THIS BOOK HAS SOME dark situations that may not be suitable for everyone. If you want a list of trigger warnings you can find them on my website http://jamiespicerauthor.com[1]

If you spot any problems with the book such as grammatical errors (I edited by myself so there very well might be), or a plot hole or you have questions email me at jamiespicerauthor@gmail.com.

Thank you for reading,

Jamie

Music Playlist:

1) ALL YOUR'N- TYLER Childers
   2) This Bar- Morgan Wallen
   3) Better Together- Luke Combs
   4) You Proof - Morgan Wallen
   5) Beer Never Broke My Heart- Luke Combs
   6) Beautiful War- Kings of Leon
   7) I love this bar- Toby Keith
   8) It ain't my fault- Brothers Osborne
   9) Buckle Bunny- Roosevelt Road
   10) Bottoms up- Brantley Gilbert
   11) Bartender Song- Rehab
   12) She got the best of me- Luke Combs
   13) Redneck Woman- Gretchen Wilson
   14) Wild as Her- Corey Kent
   15) Slumber Party- Ashnikko
   16) Dance her home- Cody Johnson
   17) Watermelon Crawl- Tracy Bird
   18) Break Up in a Small town- Sam Hunt
   19) Pony-Ginuwine
   20) Pillowtalk- Zayne

Dedication:

This book is dedicated to rekindled loves, barflies, buckle bunnies, country girls who love country boys, and to the angels in the rafters and the devils controlling the bulls.

Follow Me:

My Website: Jamiespicerauthor.com[1]
Instagram: jamiespicer.author[2]
Facebook: Jamie Spicer Author[3]
Tiktok[4]

---

1. https://jamiespicerauthor.godaddysites.com/

2. https://www.instagram.com/jamiespicerauthor

3. https://www.facebook.com/profile.php?id=100091286047284&mibextid=ZbWKwL

4. https://www.tiktok.com/@jamiespicerauthor?_t=8c0ldx359TO&_r=1

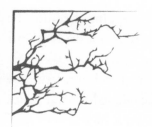

Chapter One

Remington

T he dirt and gravel spit out under my tires as I fly down the old dirt road to my father's house. I haven't been to this place in over ten years. Stress has wrecked my nerves. My hands are sweaty and my lunch seems to want to come back up. The day I left for college and finally got out of this backwoods Eastern Kentucky town, I swore I would never be back.

The dilapidated house comes into view and I swear it takes everything in me from turning around and high tailing it back to Ohio. *I can leave once I get everything squared.* I repeat to myself each time my anxiety kicks in and I feel like I'm being sucked back into this hell hole.

The house is in shambles, the once white paint is now shabby and peeling, the front screen door looks like it's off its hinges, slapping against the house because of the light breeze and there's wood haphazardly nailed to a front window. A nice, new silver Nissan is shining in the driveway and a tall, slender, older man wearing a suit and eye glasses is on the porch. Both the car and the man seem to be out of place in front of this decrepit shack. I pull my turquoise blue truck into the space beside the new vehicle, my keys clinking together as I turn off the engine. I take a deep breath and blow it out slowly. "Here we go!" I mutter to myself as I open the driver's door and swing my feet out onto the rocky drive-way.

"Remington Parker? Is that you?" The man on the porch asks in his Kentucky accent, his southern drawl drips from his lips like molasses.

"Yes sir, I'm Remmy Parker. You must be the lawyer I spoke to on the phone about my father's estate," I say, as I shorten the distance between us, being cautious about where I am stepping, because the porch looks unsafe. A gust of wind plasters my blue sun dress against my form and I catch the man eyeing my exposed legs.

"Hi, I'm Mr. Jones," he says, as he reaches his hand out, I rub my palm down my dress to remove the sweat, before taking his hand shake. "There is no reason to dilly dally out here," he says, as he reaches out of his pocket and hands me a set of keys.

My hands tremble as I take the keys from him and make quick work of side stepping to the door and opening the broken screen and unlocking the deadbolt. Unsure of why my father would need a deadbolt, it's not like he had anything of value inside, it was more than likely used to keep his secrets from escaping. I promised myself I'd never come back here. Yet, here I am.

The door creeps open, revealing nothing has changed inside the house, other than some additional furniture. Although some things have changed, it is most definitely the place of my nightmares. I quickly make my way to sit down on the faded flannel plaid couch and point at the chair. The chair I was never allowed to sit in. The chair that belonged to my father, his throne, because he always thought himself a king. The lawyer raises an eyebrow at me and looks suspicious as he takes a seat in the chair. He places a leather briefcase on his knees and removes a manilla folder from it.

"Aren't most things done electronically these days?" I ask, as I see the mess of the file.

"I'm an old man, Miss Parker, I ain't good with computers and never had an issue with paperwork," he replies by handing me a stack of papers. "Here's a copy of your father's death certificate and his will. As you know your father paid for his own funeral before he died, so no amount of his funeral will come out of the money that is willed to you. Mr. Parker had $134,675 in his bank account at the time of his death. I have emptied and closed the account and have a check for the amount.

I'll need you to sign for it." My heart stutters at the unexpected extent of the sum.

"He bestowed upon you this house, the twenty acres of land and all of his personal belongings." He pulls out another sheet of paper and he marks an x on the papers where I'm to sign. "Also, here is your deed to the Blue Moon Saloon. Your dad owned 49% and was a silent partner. 51% is owned by Beaufort Williams." He digs into the pocket of his blazer and retrieves an ink pen, his handshakes as he hands me the items.

"My father owned part of a bar?" I practically choke on the words as my eyes open wide with shock. "And Bubba Williams owns the other half?" Fuck. My. Life. This is not happening. "This is unexpected and overwhelming."

I slouch down into the sofa as the acid again rises to my throat. My mind tries to wrap around the information Mr. Jones has given me, but he keeps rattling off more things, as if he is in a hurry.

Noticing the expressions on my face, he offers an explanation; "Your father changed after you left Remington, he sobered up, and helped people in this town, we all came to care about him. You missed out on a lot of things being gone." He watches me as I sign the papers and he deposits them back into his briefcase. The old man stumbles as he stands up hastily from the chair and makes his way to the door. "Now that you own part of the bar, you might want to go talk to Bubba, the Moons open tonight." Placing his hand on the door knob, he turns to me and tells me goodbye and goodluck closing the door behind him leaving me with my memories and the remains of my father's life.

Beaufort "Bubba" Williams. Fuck. I wish I never had to hear his name again. Even though I now own this land, the small fortune, the house and part of a saloon, none of it compares to the sinking feeling I get realizing that he is now part of my life.

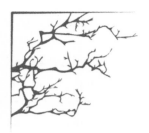

Chapter Two

Bubba

"**H**ey Bubba!" The voice of Talbert Smith booms over the "You Proof" by Morgan Wallen blaring from the bar's jukebox that is nestled in the corner.

"What's up Tal?"

"Guess what fire-haired woman I saw speeding up the Parkers drive way today." My eyes meet his, hopefully hiding my true emotions from my face as I hand him a bottle of beer. "The look on your face says you didn't hear about Miss Remington Dakota Parker driving her fine ass back to town."

"What's that got to do with me?" I ask, even though I know the answer and so does he, every mother fucking thing. I push down any emotion as I wipe a wet spot on the bar

"Your old use-to-be back in town, her daddy's death might have her needing a shoulder to cry on." He laughs as he dusts off his shoulder. "Or a dick to console her and make her forget all her troubles."

"Then why would she come to you, last I heard, straight out of Melissa Taulbee's mouth was you had a cock the size of a toddler." I laugh and walk to the back of the bar. Once I am away from prying eyes, I take a minute to get my heart calmed down. It was going to be okay, so what if Remmy is back in town, I knew sooner or later I would have to see Remington. After her father's passing, I knew she would be willed his part ownership of the bar, but I had ignored it until now. The last time I laid eyes on Remington Parker, I was only eighteen. I am a man now, I can deal with this. I can handle it. I pull at the length of my beard, my go-to habit when I get nervous and upset. I know I cannot fucking handle it, but I will pretend I can. As the beginning chords to Stephen Wesley's "Cowgirl" comes on, it drags me out of my self-induced haze. I throw my bar towel in the dirty hamper and come back to the front of the bar.

"Got a live wire for ya tonight." Samantha, my friend and bartender, greets me and nods her head in the direction of the mechanical bull. A cute blonde thing with a denim skirt and a bandana tube top, her outfit not really appropriate for riding is staring at me and pats the back of the bull, she's ready for me alright.

Not one to say no to a pretty blonde, I quickly make my way to the bullpit, dodging couples that are line dancing. Once I'm beside the bull, I place my hand on my black stetson and tilt my chin, a smile covering both of our faces, "Ma'am" I say, in a deep voice playing up the whole cowboy image. I then jump on the bull.

I haul her up, she straddles the bull with her back to its head, facing me. I place my hands on her thighs and give them a little squeeze as the bull starts off slowly, music pours from the loudspeakers and the mechanical bull begins to gently gyrate. She gazes at me, her eyes fill with a mixture of excitement and fear. I jump up with the practiced ease reminiscent of a surfer popping up on his board when he's about to catch a wave.

The mechanical monster bucks and moves and I hold onto a rope on the rafters. The bull sets my cock directly at eye level with the cute blonde and I shake my crotch at her causing her to laugh and shake her head, but she lets me grab her head as I move it towards my crotch. I jump behind her and pull her on me, making our movements sexual and sensual.

I turn her to face me in a quick expertise movement and pull her close so that she is on my lap. I place my arms under her legs and lift her in the air as I thrust forward mimicking sex in an overzealous display. The patrons go wild with hoots and hollering. After a few exaggerated lunges I turn her around so she is flat on her stomach and smack her ass. I pull the red and white bandana from my back pocket and wrap it around her throat and carefully and sensually pull her back up against me where I get close enough to her to look as if I'm kissing her neck. Then I release the bandanna and shove her down forward again. I smack her ass one last time, bending her over the front of the bull, before I toss her over to land into the soft rubber padding that surrounds the bullpit.

Her hand grazes my ass and I feel her put something into my back pocket, obviously it's her number. The little minx must have had this all planned out.

It's times like this that makes me love my job, fun times and the perks, like getting hot ladies' numbers. I love meeting new people, hanging out with the regulars, drinking and dancing and I love doing my routine on the bull. I love this bar. I put all my money, all my blood, sweat and tears into it. I realize that none of this could even have been possible without Meryl helping me buy this place. I will forever be grateful for his help.

I get hand shakes, hugs, hell even a few kisses on my cheek as I make my way back to the front. The blonde's phone number is already forgotten and will probably get washed with my pants the next time I do laundry.

I go behind the bar to grab myself some water and slide beside Sam who is making drinks for a group of college age guys. She side eyed me as I took a long pull of the bottle. "A red head came in here asking about you here a few minutes ago," she says, as she hands out a shot of whiskey.

"Oh yeah? What did she want?" I say, as I finish what's left in my water bottle.

"Hold on, Let me grab my notes, so I can give you the details exchanged. I mean I'm not your secretary, I don't know, I pointed to the bull and she looked pissed and left. I've never seen her before, you might catch her."

Samantha smiles an evil smile because she knows who she is. Hell, everyone does. Everyone knows how she left town, left her father, and left me.

It didn't take me long to decide that I needed to go after her, I need to get it over with so I do.

"Damn it, Sam, I'll be back."

"Do you want me to make my notes into a powerpoint for ya?" She takes a shot while grabbing a drink with the other hand.

I throw my hand up in the air and give her the one finger salute, letting her know what I think about her smart assed comments.

"Good luck!" She says, as I walk out into the dark, to find the girl who broke my heart.

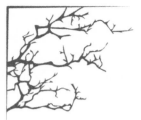

Chapter Three

Remington

When I walked into the Blue Moon Saloon, it was packed, people were shoulder to shoulder . The faint smell of sweat, cigarettes and saw dust was in the air. The music was blasting from the speakers, a young drunk girl stumbles passed me sloshing liquor on my shoe.

As I wait for the cute purple haired bartender to notice me, I can't help but to take in my surroundings. For a small town country bar, it sure is busy. Luckily, it's large enough to accommodate this enormous crowd. It's your typical Kentucky honky tonk with a longhorn along the wall with a bra thrown over it, black and white photos are in different sized frames and an American Flag is hung in honor of the veterans that frequent, I'm sure. The unfinished red brick walls give it an unintentional appeal that big city bars pay large amounts of money to achieve.

When the bartender finally notices me, she nods her head in my direction almost as if she knows me from somewhere, but I've never seen her before. She immediately sways towards me and I can't help but to notice how hot she is with just the right amount of cleavage hanging out of her black Blue Moon Saloon tank top, a pair of cut off jean shorts, black cowgirl hat, chaps and cowboy boots. Her name tag says Samantha and she's fucking adorable.

"What can I get ya?" She asks, with a smile.

I Take a look around my surroundings,"Um, Beaufort Williams?" I say, in a nervous voice.

Samantha raises her tattooed arm and motions to the back of the Saloon. A crowd is gathered watching a man and a woman on a mechanical bull. A breath catches in my throat when I realize who the man is and what exactly he is doing. It's Bubba and he is basically dry humping a hot blonde for everyone to see. Anger immediately replaces my surprise and I am pissed off in an instant. I have no idea why I care about what I see, but I definitely do, and that realization makes me even more enraged. Bile burns the back of my throat making me want to vomit. I need to get out of here before I actually decorate the floor with my lunch, making a bigger jackass out of myself than I already have.

Mumbling thanks to Samantha, I quickly escape the scene. I need fresh air and to not see my new business partner basically acting out a porn on a mechanical bull. I should have known better than to come here. I could have just called, but a part of me didn't believe that Bubba could be in my life again, so I had to see it for myself. I grapple for the door handle and quickly throw myself out onto the sidewalk. Luckily, no innocent pedestrians are harmed in my desperation to flee my past. The sidewalk is clear, only the moon is shining down on it as I speed walk to my car. The metal on the roof is hot, but I don't care as I rest my head on it and close my eyes. I need a moment to gather my thoughts and calm myself down, to curse my dad and to rethink my life choices. I shouldn't have left Ohio, I could have just talked to the lawyer on the phone and he would take care of everything. It's been ten long years since I have left this town and perhaps I should have made it another ten. I do some meditative breathing techniques and it slowly releases the tension from my muscles. *I can do this. I can just talk to the lawyer and have him handle everything. I will sell the house and my part of the bar and leave this town and put it in my rear view mirror forever.*

I had just lifted my head from the car when a large hand grabbed my bicep.

"Get your hands off me!" I scream, bracing myself for combat.

The hand abruptly releases as I whip around. Bubba's expression blanches as he holds up his hands and takes a step back. "Sorry," he quickly supplies, "Samantha said you were looking for me."

My heartbeat slowly returns to normal, but my anger only rises. "That was before I seen you dry fucking a blonde on the bull, is that how you have been managing our bar? If so, then your managerial skills need work," I say, as I glare at him in his eyes.

His sexy beard cannot hide the smile that forms on his full lips. He has the audacity to laugh, the deep rumbling goes all the way to my core. "It's all for shits and giggles, for fun, ya remember how to have fun right Remington?"

Needing to make another hasty escape, I grab my key fob out of my pocket and click the unlock button. "It's Remmy. Not Remington," I say, as I hustle myself behind the wheel. "There's a time and place for fun, not at work, not in front of the employees." I slam the door, but roll down the window. "You should know better than anyone, Beaufort, what kind of fun I can get into."

I start the car to leave but then he grips the door with his large hand. "Why'd you come here tonight, Remmy?" He folds his massive frame enough to look me in the eyes, with a voice low and full of inquiries. The smell of spices, oranges and pine hits my nostrils. Its an intoxicating concoction of old memories and late nights in the back of his pick up truck

"I came to see my saloon," I say, because I know the words will cut him like a dagger. I can tell I hit the target they intended, because all of a sudden he stands up, and crosses his arms stretching the material of his shirt over his humongous biceps, his face showing only annoyance.

"It's my saloon, and I can have sex on top of the bar if I wanted to," he says, his face is like granite, but his eyes burn with defiance.

Apparently, he knows I'm not over him as hard as I portray. "You're going to have to keep it in your pants because as of today, it is now our saloon and the only way you can service customers at the bar is by pouring them drinks." Needing to get the last word, I put the car into drive and step on the gas. In my wake, I leave behind the legacy my father left me and the man I left because of my father.

Chapter Four

Bubba

Remington knew what she was doing when she walked into my bar tonight. She loves fucking with me, always has. The juxtaposition of the fury and arousal I get from seeing Remington for the first time in ten years has really thrown me for a loop. I don't know if I want to choke her or fuck her, but I have a feeling a combination of both is the only way I can figure out how to deal with these conflicting emotions. I am wrestling with these thoughts as I open up the heavy steel doors to the saloon.

The music is thumping, the walls are shaking from the bass, everyone is still partying so I ignore all the patrons and storm into my office, and reach for my hidden bottle of Blanton's Silver Edition and pour me a drink, hiding from the rest of the world, under the guise of doing inventory. I am so wrapped up in my thoughts of anger and self loathing of a woman that broke my heart ten years ago that a couple of hours pass. I stumble as I stand up, swaying toward the door, I rest my hand on the knob and my feeble attempt at opening it, makes me realize how much I must have drunk. The noise is still at ear bleeding levels but I stumble to the bar. I clutch the microphone in my sweaty hands, my words coming out as a jumbling mess. "Last call for alcohol. You ain't gotta go home, but you can't stay here. Pay your tabs, tip the buckle bunnies and the bartenders. It's time to go!" My announcement pulls a groan from the crowd.

Buckle bunnies are what we call our female servers. I know that usually a "buckle bunny" is a degrading term for women who like to entertain bull riders. Here though, it's all out of fun and the ladies that work for me don't mind it and would gladly speak up if they did. Hell, they are the ones that asked to wear the booty shorts. They all wear the same uniform: a cowboy hat, booty shorts (or black pants), chaps, a Blue Moon Saloon tee-shirt and a pair of cowboy boots. The bunnies can choose whether they want to wear the pants or the shorts, but most opt for the shorts since customers seem to tip better when they wear them. We don't put up with any disrespect to our employees and we have bouncers, rather large muscled guys that reinforce our policies. The men were outfitted in similar jeans, a blue moon tee-shirt, cowboy hat and boots. We had them wearing booty shorts, but the customers rioted so we decided to keep it casual in jeans. We are a country bar after all. The bull pit closes down while Jacob cleans the pit, the bunnies clean tables and customers pile out. It takes a minute, but the customers finally leave. Leaving us to do our chores.

"Drive safely, call an Uber or Lyft," I call out, as I start closing up the bar with Samantha.

"You okay?" She gazes up at me as she wipes down the bar.

"Good as gold, my friend," I say, lifting a large bag of trash out of the can. "What could be wrong?"

Her brown eyes catch me in a death stare, because she knows I'm lying. "I don't know, you looked kinda pissed when you came back in. Did the one who got away bust your balls?" Her smugness shows cause she is smart as fuck and knows me so well. She is scrubbing the oak bar top so aggressively you would have thought it told her a bad your mama joke.

"Possibly," I groan, as I start to walk away.

"Well boss, whatcha going to do about it?"

"Invests in a jock strap." I wink, stumbling through the bar with the bag of empty bottles to take back to the dumpster.

"Also, put up a wall around my heart," I mutter, to myself as I sling the trash bag into the dumpster and shake my head. She came into my life again after ten years and obliterated the wall I had built up.

The bar is swept and mopped and the register is counted as Samantha hands me the profit from tonight. The attitude that she gives me thankfully, is in the form of an annoyed look instead of her sharp tongue. I stroll down the long hallway to my office, somehow I manage it still feeling the effects of the alcohol I drank earlier and put the money in the safe so I can deposit it on Monday.

The workers yell bye as they leave, the bouncers walk the females to their vehicles, and I hike out behind them, the metal door clanking as I lock it behind me. Even though the bar is closed for the night, I still have my work cut out for me. Now I just have to decide how I can talk Remington into selling me her part of my bar.

I borrowed money from Meryl Parker when I decided to open the bar seven years ago. Instead of lending it to me he wanted to be a silent partner. We were never close until after Remington left, then we became close. With him being a silent partner it let me run the bar as I wanted. I built the bar into what it is today and no matter the past, no matter how much I loved Remmy Parker, she wasn't going to take it away.

I CRAWL INTO MY BED, my thoughts are heavy as I lie here and before I know it, it's four in the morning. Since I can't sleep, I flip through the TikTok. Tiktok is a social media app where people make videos and lip-synch songs. A lady singing about buckle bunnies pops up on my for you page and the coincidence is she mentions Kentucky. I download the song "Buckle Bunny" by Tanner Adell, thinking it might be a good song for the bar and send it to Samantha asking what she thinks. It was a few minutes later when she responds:

Samantha: Why are you still awake? It is a kick ass song. Don't expect me to dance to it though. See ya tomorrow night.

Me: I never do. Goodnight Samantha.

I ignore her question, she doesn't need to know that I have Remmy on the brain.

Samantha: Night boss.

I put my phone on the charger and turned over hoping to get emerald green eyes and red hair far from my mind.

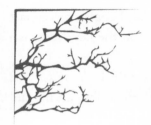

Chapter Five

Remington

I'm dead asleep when the rumble of a lawn mower jolts me out of bed, tripping over my sheets, I race to the window to look out. The sun has barely stretched over the horizon and I yawn as I peek out the window to the neighbors yard across the street. I should have known, I ran down the stairs and into the front yard throwing my arms up and waving them around trying to get the attention of the man on the riding lawn mower. Finally, catching his gaze, he turns the key on the lawn mower and the noise stops, leaving me still shouting.

"What the hell do you think you're doing, Bubba?" I scream, at the top of my lungs. "It's six in the morning hell even the roosters aren't up crowing yet!" I'm pissed and I am about to give him ten years of pent up hell when he looks me up and down with amusement shining in his eyes and starts laughing.

"What the fucks so funny, you big hillbilly!" I yell. I am so mad that I don't even care that I am barefoot walking across the gravel driveway to Bubba's mother's house.

"Hey, now Remmy ain't no need for name calling. I needed to mow the grass, I have work at the shop then the bar tonight and it needs done. You are, what's so funny, your hairs piled on your head, you're wearing SpongeBob sleep shorts and an Ice Nine Kills tank top, barefoot, screaming like a banshee and wailing your arms around like one of those things at the car lot. It's fucking funny!" He exclaims, as he laughs again, and goes to start up the mower, again.

"Just stop, I will finish mowing later, I'm tired. I couldn't sleep last night, just please don't," I say as I grab his hand on the key, his touch gives me a shock and I jerk my hand away.

"Okay, but I want it done today." He climbs off the lawnmower and dusts his pants legs off. "Guess I'll be seeing you." He walks past me and jumps into his old red Ford truck.

"Fuck," I say, to myself as I head back home, wash my feet off because they were covered in dirt and grass and climb back into bed.

A FEW HOURS LATER, I wake up to the sunshine coming into my window. I hop out of bed and throw some clothes on, then go downstairs to the big kitchen. The kitchen, unlike other rooms of the old house, has been updated with new stainless steel appliances, which is nice. I start the coffee maker and look in the refrigerator for food. There's not much to choose from, which means I'll have to go grocery shopping. I open the milk to see if it's good and my nostrils are affronted with the aroma of rotted milk. I slam the lid back on and pitch it in the trash. Then I start removing all the food that could be spoiled or out dated into the trash. The fridge is now empty and my stomach is growling. I pour a cup of coffee and check the cupboards for anything I can eat quickly when I see a box of cherry pop tarts. Booya! I climb onto the counter and grab the delicious toaster pastries and rip them open. Black coffee and cherry pop tarts, breakfast of champions. I eat the pastries and down my coffee. Time to go mow the fucking grass.

Chapter Six

Bubba

I knew waking her up mowing the lawn was going to get her mouth started this morning. I have smiled and laughed all day picturing her yelling and flailing her arms around, trying to get me to stop. Little does she know the lawnmower was about out of gas, so she will have some issues when she goes to finish mowing. Remmy was hot though, her small shorts barely covering her ass, showing off her rounded hips and stomach. Her belly button peeking out from under her tank top, and her cleavage showing off her immaculate large tits. I shake those thoughts out of my head as I put on the tire to Mr. Ausby's Chevy truck.

For the last few years I've worked here as a mechanic and ran the bar, the bar only being open on Friday and Saturday nights. I needed the finances from both places to get Blue Moon up and going. I was about to ask Mr. Parker to buy his part when he passed away and now unfortunately, Remmy owns his part and now I have to persuade her to sell me her share. How hard could it be? I mean I'm sure she's not wanting to stay in town any longer than necessary, so hopefully she will accept an offer, finish up her business here and I can go back to living my life pretending she doesn't exist. It's easier that way, easier not to think about the pain, the hurt and the heartbreak she has caused me. It's better to pretend, I tell myself as I walk into the lobby to get the keys for the next car that needs worked on.

MY PHONE PINGS AS SOON as I walk into my small house.

Unknown: You could have told me the lawn mower needed gas.

Unknown: Your mom said that she missed you coming by this morning.

Unknown: That's how I got your number, you arrogant ass.

Me: What did I say about the name calling Remington? That's not lady like.

Unknown: Remmy. My name is Remmy. Also, me flipping the bird at the phone is very unlady-like. I've never claimed to be a lady.

Me: No you haven't. So, did you get it mowed?

Unknown: Yes, and your mom missed me terribly. Said she's so happy I'm back in town. She said that after I left you never were the same. Guess I'm the reason you wanted nothing to do with me after I left. Seems like you left out a few things in your side of your story Beaufort.

Me: What did you tell her?

Unknown: Wouldn't you love to know?

Me: Yes.

After fifteen minutes she never responded back. Fuck, I need a shower and Remmy not to start bringing up shit from the past. I turn on the shower, the water heating up, the fog filling the bathroom and I undress and step inside. The heat of the water instantly relaxes my muscles. I pour the bodywash in my palm and begin to wash my tired body. I wrap my hand around my dick and instantly my mind goes to Remmy in her mixed matched sleeping clothes and how it hung on her body, I pictured what it felt like to have her body pressed under mine, it's been ten long years but I can still remember what it felt like to touch her, what she sounded like, the taste of her mouth and her cunt. No words can express how good her tight pussy felt clamped around me.

In no time, I was chasing my release and washing the evidence from my stomach and hand.

Don't get me wrong, I've slept with other women after Remmy left. They were meaningless and fun, they weren't close to anything I felt for Remmy and I hated that. I hated that she, after all this time, still had control over my mind, body and feelings. I wash my shaggy auburn hair and climb out of the shower, groom my beard and get ready for Saturday night at the Blue Moon Saloon.

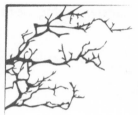

Chapter Seven

Remington

I look in the mirror at my outfit of the night. *Heads are going to turn tonight,* I think to myself as I splash some perfume on me and apply another layer of lipstick. I put on my white cowboy hat and slip on my matching boots. I grab my wallet and my keys and head out the door, time for Beaufort to realize what he has missed these last ten years.

I pull up to the bar and the music is already blasting, the car lot is full and there isn't anywhere to park so I park across the street and make my way into the bar.

The same girl is bartending that was there yesterday and she smiles at me as I saunter up to the bar, "What can I get ya, honey?"

"A Jack and Coke please Samantha," I say, smiling back at her. Gosh, she really is so darn cute with a bright smile. I hope we can be friends.

"Here ya go sweetie. You looking for Bubba?" She sets the drink in front of me on a napkin.

"No, but put this on his tab." I kill the drink and put the glass back on the bar.

An old guy wearing a veterans baseball cap with a snaggle tooth hands Samantha a fifty dollar bill, and she climbs up on the bar sitting in front of him, she has a glass of water and a shot glass full of clear liquor. She leans forward and whispers something in the guy's ear and he smiles wide and shakes his head yes. The next thing I know he downs the shot, she throws the glass of water in his face and hauls back her hand and smacks him as hard as she can. For a second the customer looks stunned, but then he smiles up at her and laughs, she kisses him on the cheek and goes back behind the counter.

"Hurricane shot," she says and shrugs her shoulders, causing me to laugh. "I get to keep the fifty."

"YOU GET FIFTY DOLLARS to throw water in people's faces and then slap them?" I am astonished I have never heard of a hurricane shot before.

I move closer to the dj station and ask him to play a song for me and then I go talk to the bull guy and ask him if I could ride next and if he minded to ride with me.

"Anything for you darlin'," he replies, as a smirk crosses my lips.

The start of a fast paced country song begins playing and I take off my shoes and head into the bullpen. I jump on and get my bearings as I get situated on the mechanical bull, my legs wrapped around the huge piece of machinery and my feet gripping it. I shake my head that I'm ready when it starts to buck but in a few seconds Jacob is on there grabbing my hips and pulling me into him. I hold onto him as I turn around to face him and wrap my legs around his waist, he pulls me up and down over his lap as if he is fucking me, I'm not going to lie, it is quite hot and a huge turn on. Plus, Jacob is hot as fuck. Jacob stands up and takes a drink from one of the buckle bunnies standing close to the pen and he drinks the liquid then grabs my hair pulling my head back as he lets the liquid flow from his mouth, down his lips into my mouth and I swallow it whole. That is one of the sexiest fucking things I have ever done, and as I'm about to stand up on the bull, it stops and standing at the controls is a pissed off Beaufort with his hands on his hips. I smile up at Jacob and tell him not to worry about it, and I hop off the bull and walk to where my boots are and put them back on.

"What the fuck do you think you are doing Remington?" Bubba asks, as I make my way back to the bar.

"Whatever the fuck I want to do!" I reply and signal Samantha to bring me another Jack and Coke.

"You just show up in my bar, tell the dj to play whatever you want, dry fuck Jacob and let him spit in your mouth?" His face is red and a vein starts to poke out of his forehead.

"I most certainly did, it's no different than what you did with that blonde on there yesterday," I state, as I took a sip of my drink.

"I'm thinking about asking him out, he is a very handsome man." I smile, and take another drink and notice Bubba balling his hands up in a fist.

"Owners can't date employees, Remington. Sorry, about your luck. Unless you want to sell me your part of the bar, then you can date anyone here, even Cletus," he says, pointing to an old man that is sitting by the door.

"I'm not selling shit Beaufort, so I guess for the next twenty years you better settle in and expect me here riding the bull, choosing music and hell I might even dance on the bar with the buckle bunnies." I laugh as I finish my drink and move out on the dance floor and start dancing as Bubba follows me.

"I thought you wanted to leave here as soon as possible," he says, as he grabs my arm.

"I never said that, besides this is the most fun I've had in years, a girl could get used to this." I raise my finger to make a circle, meaning the bar.

A slow song starts and Bubba grabs my waist and pulls me close to him. "Don't fuck this up for me Remmy, this is my life, I've put all of me into this saloon. Don't fuck it up for me." A pleading look enters his eyes and he truly believes that I want to hurt him, to take away the bar from him. I can't believe he truly believes I'm capable of such a thing.

I step back from his embrace and look him in the eyes. "I'm not taking anything away from you Beaufort. I promise." I walk away and out the front door into the cool night air.

Chapter Eight

Bubba

For the second night in a row, I went chasing after Remington. She wasn't far from the door when I caught her and turned her to face me.

"What are you planning on doing, Remington? Are you going to stay in town? You're gonna sell your daddy's place and move back to Ohio? What's your plans? I need to know. I need to prepare myself for whatever destruction comes from you being back in town."

I didn't mean to sound harsh, but I had not prepared for her to just walk back in my life like ten years and heartbreak didn't happen, like everything is fine and that night years ago didn't happen, because I can't let it go. I can't and I need to know what hell my life is going to be thrown into so I can mentally prepare.

Remmy looks me in the eyes, her emerald eyes are sad and she whispers. "I don't know Bubba, I don't know what I want to do or what I need anymore. I am lost." She pulls from my arms and spins around and walks off. I understand that, I felt the same way the day she left this town, like my whole world was crumbling. I was hurt and left to wallow in my own pain.

"You need to figure it out!" I say again harshly and start to turn around to go back into the saloon.

"I never meant to hurt you, Beau. I honest to God didn't, but I had to leave, being here was killing me and it was suffocating me." She says to me and I just nod my head and open the saloon door. I knew that. I also knew I wasnt enough for her to want to stay. I wasn't good enough for her, believe me I understood it all too well.

I didn't say anything to Jacob about the stunt on the bull with Remmy, it's not like he would have known that as far as anyone around here knew she was off limits and co-owner of the bar. He apologized anyway, knowing something wasn't right by the way I acted. I guess like a caveman. It's a wonder I didn't bang on my chest, like a gorilla. My girl. Her mine, not yours. Seeing them on the bull like that and her drinking alcohol from his mouth kinda disgusted me and well kinda made me wish it was me doing it to her. This love/hate thing I have going on for her has to stop, she is off limits for everyone at the bar including me, especially me. My heart cannot take another crash from the bulldozer known as Remington Parker.

We close down the bar and I pull out my phone and send a message to Remmy.

Me: You're forgiven. I'll give you $150,000 for your share of the bar. It's all the money I have, it's yours, just sign the papers. Think about it.

Remmy: I'm not selling the bar, keep your money. Goodnight Beaufort.

Well, fuck. My. Life.

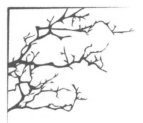

Chapter Nine

Remington

I jumped out of bed as soon as my alarm went off. I have a helluva lot to do today. First things first, a hot shower. As I enter the bathroom, I turn on the faucet and wait for the water to warm up while I undress. Before stepping into the shower, I check the water temperature with my hand to ensure it's not scalding hot. The steam envelops me as I step in. I am satisfied with the soothing sensation of the hot water cascading over my skin.

I reach for the shampoo and work it into my hair, relishing the feeling of my fingers massaging my scalp. After rinsing, I repeat the process with the conditioner, savoring the sweet aroma of strawberries as it permeates the air. Next, I grab my favorite body wash and lather it onto my sponge, carefully scrubbing every inch of my body within reach.

I hate to look at my body. The scars that remain after all these years, the memories associated with them, and how small and afraid they make me. I shake my head, ridding the dark thoughts away as I turn off the water and grab the towel that's hanging on the shower door. As I step out of the shower, the doorbell rings once, and then I hear footsteps departing. *Must be a delivery*, I think as I load my toothpaste on my brush and brush my teeth. After I use the bathroom, comb, and dry my hair, I dress in jeans and a tee shirt. It's an old George Jones tee shirt that belonged to Bubba, and I kept it all these years. I stole it from him one night after making out in his truck. It's been my favorite shirt since then. I put on socks and Nikes and walk down the stairs and open the front door.

There's a vase of pink carnations and a card.

Remmy,

I'm sorry for the way I acted last night. Let me make it up to you. Seven tonight, I'll pick you up.

Xoxo, Bubba

I couldn't help it, I smiled and my stomach did nervous fluttering as I lifted the vase and brought it into the house.

I place the vase on the kitchen counter and pull out my phone.

Me: Thank you for the flowers, they are beautiful. I don't think we should meet up at seven.

Bubba: You're welcome. What are you scared of? Come on just one night.

Me: One night. See you at seven.

I look up house painters on Google and find several businesses in my area and call a few for estimates. I need to get the ball rolling on fixing up this house and clearing out my father's things.

I still have to go to the grocery store and buy a few personal things I need. So, I grab my purse and head out the door to get some errands taken care of. It's not much but it's a start. I can get the house painted and I'll start going through things I want to donate, sell or keep tomorrow.

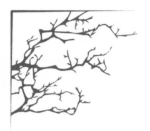

Chapter Ten

Bubba

I left work early at the shop to prepare for my date with Remmy. I transformed the bar's dance floor with a stunning array of twinkling lights and flickering candles, creating an enchanting ambiance. At the center of the room, I placed a table with a flickering candle, inviting us to share a romantic dinner. I had lovingly prepared a feast of savory short ribs, creamy mashed potatoes, and a crisp side salad. Soft, warm rolls and a decadent pecan pie from the bakery downtown completed our meal. After showering and donning my finest attire, a sleek black long-sleeved button-down, my favorite pair of wranglers, and polished black cowboy boots. I took one final look in the mirror, running my hand through my hair and beard with a grin.

I check everything again and made sure it was just right, a bout of nerves hitting me suddenly. I have no clue why, it's only Remmy. I've been on hundreds of dates with her, I've touched and tasted the most intimate parts of her, so why the nerves? I shake them off and grab my keys, locking up the bar behind me.

Remmy lives only a few minutes from town, across the street from my moms house. So, in no time I pull up into her driveway and choke up on what I see standing on her porch.

Remmy's hair is down, curled into waves that framed her face, her makeup is light except for her lips. They are painted a bright red and I can't help but imagine what her lips would look like wrapped around my cock. I adjust myself as I climb out of my truck and open the door for her as she runs to my truck her short black dress flowing in the wind, showing over her shapely thighs and legs and how hot she is wearing those high heeled shoes and for a second I picture her riding me only wearing them.

"Beaufort," she says, as she kisses me on the cheek and I take her hand to help her into my truck.

"Remington," I say, as I close the door and climb back into the driver's side of the truck.

"Where are we going?" She turns her head to look at me and I notice a sparkle in her green eyes.

"It's a surprise. I really hope you like it," I say, as I pull out onto the main road and head back to the saloon.

The drive is silent, not awkward, just quiet, but I can tell that she's nervous, she keeps wringing her hands and biting her lower lip. I take my finger and tap her lip so she stops biting them. She laughs gently. "I don't know why I'm nervous."

"It's ok, I am too Remmy," I say, as I pull into the Blue Moon's parking lot and go around to help her out.

"Our date is here?" She asks, as she lets me guide her to the door so I can unlock it and let us in.

"Yes, I've cooked for us." I step back and let her walk into the bar where I hear her gasp. She spins around and looks at the lights and the battery operated timer candles. I've lit the whole bar and the table that was set up in the middle of the dance floor.

"It's so pretty. Like thousands of little stars, Bubba," she exclaims, as she walks up to the chair and I pull it out for her. The dishes are covered and I uncover them so we can eat our meal. The smell of the meat and potatoes permeates the room. I pour her a glass of red wine and grab a bottle of beer from the cooler behind the bar and sat down across from her. Man, she is so pretty the candles flicker against her skin and hit her just right, more than pretty, Remington Parker is fucking stunning and I love the smile that has crossed her face, and I like that I'm the one who put it there.

"This is amazing Bubba really, you've gone through a lot of trouble," she says, as she takes a bite of her ribs. Her eyes pop out and a moan escapes her lips as she enjoys the food and I swear it's better than any audio of porn ever made. "I didn't know you could cook."

"You don't know much about me anymore Remmy, we are familiar strangers. Ten years is a long time. I'm not a boy anymore, I've grown up, I'm all man now," I say, and I swear I heard her reply "yes you are" in a mumble.

"You're right we are both different people than we were back then. We were silly kids, full of dreams and crazy things," She replies, taking another bite.

This time I watch as she wraps the fork with her mouth, how her lips move, the way her throat vibrates as she swallows and I think I'm going to come in my pants like a thirteen year old.

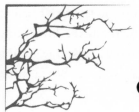

Chapter Eleven

Remington

Bubba went all out on our "date". He thinks he is sly, that he is wooing me, to try to talk me out of selling my share of Blue Moon. I know him, I know how he thinks, like most men, or boys, he thinks his cock is a magical wand that makes women lose their minds and fall victim to his games. I'm not crazy, I know how his brain operates, so I play his game. I admire the pretty lights, the delicious meal, the way those wranglers fit his tight ass. I even let him hold me close as he plays a slow song and we dance, swaying to the old country song.

His cologne is intoxicating and different from when he used to hold me in high school, a more manly scent I can appreciate. His arms are thicker, stronger, hell his whole body is, he was always broad and strong and tall. I always enjoyed his hard body against my soft, curvy, chubby one. I enjoyed him. I admired his body, but I definitely wasn't going to be swept away, with his game. No sir. Not me. I learned my lesson a long time ago.

The song comes to an end, but he doesn't let me go. Instead, he pulls me closer, a sparkle in his eyes as he bends closer to me and his lips touch mine, gently at first kissing my top lip, then bottom, then each side, my nose my forehead and back to my lips. He pressed harder, his tongue licking the seam of my lips, begging for entrance which I obliged. I open up for him, our tongues tangling, teeth clashing, a hunger coming over me I haven't felt in years. I run my hands over his shoulder, behind his head and pull him closer to me as I hear a growl escape him, he hoists me up and I wrap my legs around him. He walks me over to the bullpit, uses a free hand and clicks a switch and sets me on the bull. He puts me on the back of it and hops on the front facing me. He guides me in front of him and starts kissing me again. His hands roaming my sides, and going up under my shirt to my breast. He groans as he pulls the shirt over my head and looks at my red lace bra, a smile crosses his face.

"Fucking beautiful," he exclaims, as he starts to unlatch the clasp. My breast on full display, he bends down and starts sucking on my nipple and I know my panties are soaked.

I move my hand to his jeans and start to unbuckle them when a glass breaking noise happens at the front of the bar and a tall, skinny brunette waltzes up to the bullpen and I scramble to cover myself.

"What the fuck, Bubba?!" The little woman shouts as I look at her and realize who she is. I jump off the bull and grab my shirt.

"What the fuck is going on?!" I demand, scrambling to cover myself.

Bubba's face is white. His eye brows are scrunched up and he is pissed. "What the fuck are you doing here, Arlene?"

I look at them both confused. Knowing I just got played, a sinking feeling in my stomach.

"One of you fuckers, better tell me what's going on," I say, my hands on my hips, a scowl on my face.

Arlene walks up to Bubba and wraps her hand around his arm and looks at me like I'm trash, "Bubba and I have been together going on a few years now," she gloats, as she kisses his cheek.

"Y'all are together?" I ask, and I can feel my sanity about to snap as a guilty look comes across Bubba's face.

"We ain't together, together," he says, as he unwraps her hand from his arm. "It's never been serious."

"So you're what? Fuck buddies? Friends with benefits?" I look at Bubba and I can't stand his face, I get close to him as Arlene takes a step back with a smile across her face. "You were just going to fuck me on the bull, and then what go back home and fuck her too? You're disgusting."

"We don't liv..." He starts to say but before he can finish the sentence I rare back with all the power I have in me and punch him in his nose.

See, told ya I couldn't trust him. I think to myself.

"I was going to sign my part over to you, ya know. I was just going to give you my share. Now though, I think I love this place. I think I'm going to love my bar." I start to stroll out the door, but turn around. "See ya Friday night Beaufort," I say, as I flip him and his friend with benefits the bird, because I am a classy redneck like that.

"Fuck Beaufort. Fuck this town. Fuck my life," I scream into the darkness, as I walk to my father's house. My hand is hurting and needs iced.

Fuck. My. Life.

Chapter Twelve

Arlene

The look on Bubba's face is disheartening. Have I truly misread our relationship? Are fuck buddies really all we are? As he watches the red head walk out of the saloon, I have to admit I've never seen him look at me like that. The air is thick and my chest tightens as I take a deep breath. Heart break. Yes, that's what it is. I've known all about the red head I caught him with, he's not held back from telling me about them. The high school sweethearts, the prom king and queen and how he loved her as much as an eighteen year old could be in love. He didn't lie to me, never told me we were exclusive, never said we were more than fuck friends. I knew that.

However, it still hurts. He turns around abruptly facing me, hurt and pain written on his face, meets his eyes. I flinch, not because I'm scared he will hurt me, it's for the pain I see. Before he can say anything, I begin apologizing.

"I'm sorry Bubba, I guess I went and crossed the line. I thought we were something we obviously aren't. It's on me and I'm truly sorry. I'll talk to Remington, I will tell her I mistook our arrangement for more than it truly was," I say, as I take a step away from him.

"Arlene, I'm sorry I hurt you, I've been upfront and honest with you. You've been a good friend to me, you were there when I needed a friend and I appreciate that. I really do. But it's her, it's been her and will always be her." He runs his hands through his auburn hair, it flows through his fingers.

I choke down the tears that start to come and kiss his cheek and walk out of the Blue Moon Saloon, with my head held high and my heart crumbled into bits and pieces.

A chill comes over me as I climb into my vehicle, tears are flowing from my eyes as I wipe them away. Not five minutes down the road I see Remington Parker still walking on the side of the road, so I pull up in front of her.

"Remington," I say, getting out of my car as her wary eyes flash my way and I can see the redness as she too wipes her tears away. "I'm sorry. Listen Bubba and I are just friends, I know that now. I guess I always loved him, cared about him more than he did me and wanted something more than what he could give me. He loves you, Remmy. He's loved you since you've been kids. This is on me and I take full responsibility," I say, wiping tears from my eyes.

She stands still, tears pouring from her eyes and shakes her head. "He doesn't love me, Arlene. We have chemistry and history and that's all there is," She says as she starts to walk again.

"I told him I would apologize. I did, but let me tell you what I do know. He told me all about you, about your whirlwind high school true love, the arguments, the love, the highs and lows and how you left. It broke him. He loved you then and he loves you now. He's a good guy, he deserves happiness. So, think again if you don't think he cares about you, he does. You're a lucky girl. Now, if you want a ride back to your home, get in the car." I walk back to my car and get in and look out the window and see her moving towards the passenger seat.

Remmy opens the door and climbs in. "Thank you," she whispers, then she turns around with a large smile on her face and says. "Hey Arlene, do you need a job?"

I looked at her blankly. "Sure, what do you have in mind?" I ask, as she tells me to get out of the car and follow her in.

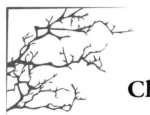

Chapter Thirteen

Bubba

I am an idiot. A fuck up. A dumb ass. Stupid. Stupid. Stupid. I take another drink from the bottle of Jack, I've been chugging since Arlene walked out. Two women. I've hurt two women tonight. A good friend that's always been there for me, she's been a person I could vent to, a friend and a distraction when my life was shit. I should have treated her better, I'm a bastard. I can admit when I'm wrong, I'm a man and that's what men do, admit to their wrongs and fix their mistakes. Arlene is a wonderful girl who deserves an amazing guy, it's just not me.

I sigh deeply, throwing back another swig as Keith Whitley's "I'm Over You," plays on the radio. Remmy. God the look of pure hatred on her face, it guts me. I don't know how I can ever get her to trust me. To believe that I'm the guy for her, to get her to stay in town. Ha, that's gone. She will definitely leave again, and there goes her ownership in Blue Moon. The person who buys it will end up being a dick, I just know it.

I really fucked up everything. Again. I pull out my phone and find Remmys name and message her.

Me: I am sorry. Please forgive me.

I stare at the screen and get nothing in response and then I pass out, my head on the bar of the Blue Moon Saloon, heart broke and pissed at myself.

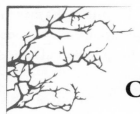

Chapter Fourteen

Remington

I look at my phone, a message from Bubba, but it's unreadable, just a bunch of jumbled letters. Great. He's trying to get my attention in any way he can. I scowl, as I put the phone back in my pocket.

"That's great, yeah I can work part time at the saloon," Arlene says, as she looks at me. "Call Samantha, have her get a hold of the bunnies, we will all meet you at the bar in the morning to practice." She grabs her purse and starts toward the door. "I really am sorry, Remmy."

"It's all good Arlene. No worries," I say, as she walks out and closes the door behind her.

I'm a wreck, I've ugly cried, laughed, and figured out just what I'm going to do. Also, the house painters are coming in the morning to start working on the house. I'm bone tired and just strip out of my clothes, figuring I can shower in the morning.

UGH! I HATE MORNINGS. The sound of trucks, men yelling and scraping wake me up.

I look out my bedroom window and see two white trucks with Higgins on the side of it. Derrick Higgins is the owner of the construction company. They usually don't do house paintings only, but I went to school with Derrick and it will be a short job for his crew members to just knock it out.

I slip on a pair of jeans and a tee shirt and go downstairs and make a pot of coffee. I check my phone and see a message saying that everyone will meet at ten at the saloon. I give her the thumbs up emoji and notice messages and calls from Bubba.

Bubba: Please talk to me.

Bubba: Answer your phone.

Bubba: Fuck, I should have made sure Arlene knew we were done before asking you on a date.

Bubba: I'm sorry.

Bubba: Are you going to ignore me now?

Bubba: Be that way then!

The last message reminded me of a toddler that didn't get his way so he is throwing a fit. When the coffee finished percolating I made myself a cup and poured some in a thermos. It's the least I could do for Derrick and his crew and grab some Styrofoam cups, some sugar and cream packets too and head outside.

There were five workers, and they seemed to have almost the house stripped of old paint already. Fuck, they are not playing around. I look around and see Derrick behind the house talking to another dark haired guy and holding out the thermos and condiments.

"Here's y'all some coffee. I appreciate you doing this for me Derrick."

He smiles as he takes the thermos. "No problem, Remmy." He looks me over his gaze flirting down my body and then looks me in my eyes. "God, woman, you sure haven't changed a bit since high school," he says, as his tongue darts out and licks his thick lips.

I place my hand on his arm and laugh. "I don't know Derrick. You can't see the dimples in my fat ass thighs," I joke.

The glint in his eyes shows me he wants to see them.

"You're like a fine wine and I bet you taste just as sweet." He pours him a cup of the coffee, black and takes a drink. "I'm sorry," he says, coming out of his flirty mood. "About your dad."

I shrug my shoulders. "Don't be Derrick, my father and I weren't close."

He shrugs his shoulders. "I'll let you get back to it," I say, as I pat his shoulder and walk away.

Derrick hasn't changed at all, still fun, flirty, and very good looking. One day he will make some woman very happy, but it's not going to be me. I finish my cup of coffee and get ready to meet the girls at the saloon. Time to put the bunnies to work and have one hell of a show Friday night.

"THEN YOU CLIMB UP LIKE this," Asa, one of the buckle bunnies says, as she shows me one of her signature moves on the bull. "Jacob will make sure that the bull is the pace and speed you need it to be. You have to trust him."

"I don't know if I can do that!" I say, as I watch her, she sits on the bull and holds her hand out to me wanting me to get on the bull with her.

"Let's give the boss a show, Remington. One that will brand on his brain." Asa maneuvers her body so that she is facing me and pulls me up on her with strength you wouldn't think she had as she looks like she is humping me and then she gets up and moves behind me, pulls my hair back into me and licks my neck as "Pour some sugar on me" comes on the jukebox. Asa then helps me up so we are both standing on the bull. She grabs the noose that's hanging there and swings her legs up on the rafters and hangs down, grabs my face and pulls my lips to her and she kisses me. Her tongue massaging mine, deep and sexy and all the others cheer. I'm not going to lie, I think my panties are soaked from my first girl on girl kiss and I ain't mad about it. Asa pulls away and I slip back down on the bull.

"Are you sure you're into men?" She winks at me and smiles as she makes her way back down from the rafters.

"I mean with a kiss like that, you have me definitely questioning my sexual preferences," I say, with a blush on my cheeks. not going to lie to myself that the kiss was hot.

I shake my head. "Okay, back from the top, let's get this dance and bull routine down," I say, as I clap my hands and we all get started on the new Friday night dance and bull routine starring Arlene and me. This time Arlene is doing the part that Asa was showing me and it took plenty of practices, but I was determined to make this hot as fuck.

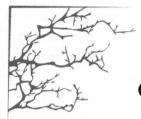

Chapter Fifteen

Bubba

It's been three days now and still no word from Remington or Arlene. Guess they are over my bullshit. I finish my work at the auto shop and go home and shower. This whole thing has been fucking with my mind and I'm seriously fucked up over what she plans to do with her part of the bar. Hopefully, she will decide to talk to me like an adult soon and we can work things out.

An hour and a half later, I walk into the Blue Moon and no one is there. Samantha or Jacob is usually already setting up and getting things ready, but there isn't a soul in sight. I message them and go and start putting the chairs off the table and start prepping the bar for drinks. Fifteen minutes before opening Samantha walks in and goes straight to the stack of aprons and puts it on and shortly after Jacob comes in with a lazy smile on his face.

"Why are y'all late?" I ask, with my hands on my hips.

Samantha smiles, and just shrugs her shoulders. "It's none of your business, I'm sorry I'm late. Won't happen again."

I look at Jacob and he has guilt written all over his face as he heads to the bull pit to get the bull ready for rides.

She starts to make sure the cooler is full as regulars start piling in. I give Tommy his bottle of bud and Henderson his gin and tonic. Then all the crowd starts coming. It's really busy. Everyone is fighting to get orders and I haven't seen one of the servers all night.

"Where's the girls?" I ask Samantha with a pissed look on my face.

"They said they will be a little late tonight, no worries." She pops the caps on seven beers and starts handing them down the bar and then lays out fifteen shots and pours them perfectly, not missing a drop.

After we take care of the orders at the bar, a song comes on the radio and someone speaks on a microphone.

"Ladies and cowboys, can we have your attention please." In comes Remmy, Arlene, Asa, and Melody from the back door and Shy and Tae come from the front.

All wearing tops that barely cover their breasts, more like sparkly bras and booty shorts with fishnet stockings, sexy boots and cowboys hats. Each girl looking fucking fantastic, then I noticed Samantha climbing over the bar her tee shirt removed and her wearing the same thing as the others. Which is shocking, because Samantha rarely participates in dancing with the buckle bunnies.

The crowd disperse to the side as the girls meet in the middle of the dance floor. The song "Slumber Party" by Ashnikko starts and they are dancing all over each other, ass slapping, bodies moving together. Remmy and Arlene practically scissoring in the middle of the dance floor and I don't know whether to be highly pissed off or highly turned on as they both get on the bull and shake their asses. Arlene goes between Remmy's legs like she's eating her pussy and I swear my cock is going to burst out of my zipper. Arlene jumps up onto the rafter and hangs down when Remmy and her kiss one of the hottest kisses I've ever laid my eyes on and I'm fucking man enough to admit, I'm jealous.

As the song comes to an end Samantha jumps back over the bar throws her tee shirt back on and starts giving out drinks like the most hottest sapphic show didn't happen here in this small country town in the middle of my country as fuck saloon.

I stood there for what felt like forever when Arlene made her way up to the bar and gave me orders to her tables as Remington sat down at the bar in front of Samantha and asked for a Jack and Coke.

"What the fuck was that, Arlene?" I say, "You don't work here!" My eyebrows drawn up I could only imagine the look on my face.

"Oh, Bubba, I do work here now. Oh and that." she wipes the side of her lip like she's drooling. "That's our new Friday night routine, do you like it?" She smiles up at me with a shit eating grin and I hand her the drinks and turn to Remmy.

"YOU. THE. BACK. NOW!" I point to Remmy and she nods her head, and downs her drink and stands up walking around the bar and weaving through people.

"What can I do for you, Beaufort?" She asks, in an overly politeness that makes my blood pressure rise.

"What was that whore show on my bull?" I just know the vein in my forehead is going to pop. "You can't just come in here hiring people and changing things. This is my bar!" I growl.

"Now Beaufort, it's not nice to slut shame. You can't get by with that these days." She smiles, and crosses her arms making her breast shoot up and almost spills them out of her shirt. Not that I'm looking, I totally wasn't.

"Eyes up here, fucker," she says, busting my ogling. "I own this bar too, or did you forget? I can do whatever the fuck I want to it and ain't shit you can do about it!"

I look her in the eye. "That's soft porn you can't do that here."

"Oh please, we were clothed you're just mad cause me and Arlene practically dry fucked all over the bar. Get over yourself. The customers loved it. We are doing it again next week." She spins around and walks out as I pick up a bottle of bourbon from the stock and throw it against the wall.

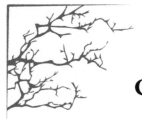

Chapter Sixteen

Remington

Bubba has been either ignoring me or giving me hateful looks all night. I'm not bothered by it at all. I laugh, flirt and help the girls get the orders out. Might as well actually help since I'm playing the part of an excited new bar owner. When the buckle bunnies songs come on, queuing them to line dance. I joined in and to be honest, it's fun. I love the atmosphere, the customers are great, and everyone is having a good time.

"Can we talk in private?" Arlene comes up to me as I'm taking empty bottles to the trash. I nod my head and motion to the back of the bar.

"What's wrong? You did awesome today by the way," I say, as I pull out a chair and sit down.

"I thought I could handle it. I thought I could pretend I didn't care about him, but I do. I can't do this Remmy, I am sorry." A tear drops from her pretty blue eyes and she wipes it away.

"It's okay. I totally understand. You don't have to do anything you don't want to do and I'm sorry I asked this of you. I just wanted Bubba to get a taste of his own medicine. I didn't stop to think of your feelings," I say as I stand up, and dig through my tips in my wallet and hand her a wad of money that more than made up for the work she did tonight. "Here take this. I'll let everyone know that you decided that you didn't want to work here."

Arlene wraps her arms around me and hugs me, taking the cash and putting it in her pocket, she walks past the back door and I go to find Bubba chatting up a voluptuous, raven haired beauty.

"Excuse me, I need him for a minute," I say, as I tap her on her shoulder and step between them. The look she gives me is pure daggers to my back. He looks almost amused though and I want to knock the smugness from his face.

"You broke her, you know?" I look him in his eyes. "She's in love with you."

"Who is? Lorelei?" He looks at me dumbfounded. "She barely knows me!" He scoffs.

"Were you born this big of an idiot or did you have some kind of brain damage in the last ten years to make you so ignorant?" I look at him and I am so mad I close my hands in fist feeling my nails dig into my palms. "Arlene. Arlene is in love with you Beaufort Williams and you fucking broke her. You hurt her so bad and you need to make it right. You need to apologize, be an adult. Be a real fucking man and right your wrongs." I shake my head as I walk back to the bar to relieve Samantha for a break and watch Bubba just stand there in the middle of the dance floor for five minutes then watch him walk out the door.

The rest of the night, I work behind the bar slinging drinks with Sam. Bubba never came back so we all worked together closing down for the night. I don't know what happened after he left. If he decided he wants to be with Arlene, or if he fixed their friendship or if she told him to go jump off Caudills' bridge. I don't know which scenario I wanted and whether or not it would bother me. I'm confused about so many things anymore, the bar, staying here or going back to my job, my friends, my apartment back in Ohio. My leave time was coming to an end so I needed to make a decision soon.

I just hope I make the best one.

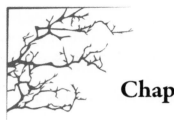

Chapter Seventeen

Bubba

How could I fix all of this bullshit? How could everything turn upside down in so little time? Every since Remington Parker came back into this fucking town, my life has been a natural disaster and I wanted to blame Remmy. Blame her for being so fucking perfect, so fucking sexy, so fucking annoying, but so fucking mine. She's always been mine, until of course the day she left. I have to make all this stuff right. I had to make things right with Arlene, but for now I want to give her space. Then hopefully, in time, we could work our issues out. I needed to make things right with Remmy, had to let her know how much I care, how much I always cared, how much I always loved her.

I pace the house floors, chugging on my fifth of Jack, pulling my hair, a cigarette hanging from my mouth. I don't even smoke usually, only when I am stressed out. I am fucking everything up, every fucking thing. I really never thought I would see her again. After Remmy left, Arlene was there for me. We were friends and after Troy Alterman her fiance was killed in a car wreck Arlene was left devastated. Her whole world crumbling, we sought comfort in each other. Both of us needing understanding and caring and a fucked up form of love. We were there for each other, in whatever way the other needed. I truly care for her and love her in a way, nothing how I felt for Remington, but in a friendly, protective way. I didn't like that I hurt her. It kills me, especially after what we've been through together.

My mind numb and my body tired. I curled up on the sofa and passed out clinging to the bottle.

"FUCK, REMMY." I MOAN as I throw her up against the wall, I grab her leg and angle her body to mine so I can enter her. Thrusting myself into her with one quick motion. Her breathing hitches as I lose myself in her.

"Harder Bubba. I need you," she moans, as she moves her head to mine, taking my mouth hungrily.

"You're mine. Only mine," I say, my lips against hers, my hand between us as I bury my dick to the hilt, rubbing her clit. Her lips slam back into mine and I feel her tightening around me as she starts to come, her teeth biting down on my bottom lip.

My eyes pop open and I look down, my hand wrapped around my length and the result of my dream on my stomach. Fuck, it had been so real. I wipe my come on my pants as I stand up. My neck is stiff and my back sore from the way I passed out on the couch. My head is busting and my mouth is full of cotton. I walk to the kitchen and start a pot of coffee before opening the big sliding door to let my geriatric black Labrador Pedro out to use the bathroom. While he does his business and my coffee brews I head to the bathroom to wash off the consequences of my nocturnal emission.

I strip my clothes off, relieve my bladder, and step into the shower turning on nothing but the hot water. Damn, the water feels so good. It heats up my bones and relaxes my muscles as I lather up and wash myself. Working out a plan to make things right with my best friend and the love of my life.

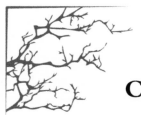

Chapter Eighteen

Remington

"You really upset Bubba, ya know?" Samantha says to me, as I wipe down tables and put the chairs up on them, so the cleaning crew can clean the floor.

"That was the point. He really upset Arlene and me too. He will get over it." I dip my dirty rag in a bucket of cleaning solution and wring it out. "I was shirtless and dry humping him like a teenager on the bull when Arlene walked in announcing they are together. It was the consequences of his own actions. He deserved it."

I shrug my shoulders and grab the bucket and take it behind the bar where I empty the dirty, smelly water and throw the rag into a dirty clothes basket.

"You know, he still loves you." Samantha's sapphire eyes look up at me. "Arlene was a friend to him, someone to lose himself in, because you weren't around."

"He doesn't love me, Sam." I inhale and let an exaggerated puff out as I take a seat at the bar. "He loved me years ago, I left him, I ran away from him, from my father, from this town. He doesn't love me, he doesn't know who I am, anymore. He didn't really know me then, he knew the "me" I showed everyone. The happy go-lucky cheerleader, the secret book lover and nerd. He didn't know me and he still doesn't." I bow my head, my heart is heavy and thoughts of my past flash before my eyes.

"You're wrong Remington. You're so very wrong. You can tell me to fuck off, but I think you still love him too or you wouldn't have came up with this little show. He hurt you, so you hurt him back." She slaps the bar in front of me. "Y'all aren't teenagers anymore, you need to talk about your shit, fix it and grow the fuck up."

I look Samantha in her eyes. "You need to practice what you preach, Samantha Justice. What's this sneaky-linking around with Jacob the bull guy?" Samantha's look went from smirking to something else, a look of confusion. "Oh yes, that's right, we all know. Maybe you should work on your shit, yourself."

Samantha turned around and grabbed a bottle of Johnnie Walker Blue label and filled us a double shot each and we down them then she filled them up again. "You are right, Remmy."

"I usually am Sam, unfortunately," I say, as I grab the bottle and guzzle it.

Chapter Nineteen

Bubba

I contacted Derrick Higgins, the guy who is working on Remmy's house. I instructed him to send me the bill for any construction work he did or needs to do. I also instructed them not to mention the work was being paid for. I call the florist and have yellow roses sent to Arlene. Yellow roses stand for friendship and that I care for her friendship. I have them sign a note saying I'm sorry for being an asshole and that I hope one day she can forgive me. I know it's not enough, I know, but I need to figure it out and hey, it's a start, right?

I have to be more creative when it comes to Remmy. She wouldn't enjoy flowers, she's never understood the tradition of guys buying girls floral arrangements for things, especially when they fuck up. She appreciates action. So that's what I'm going to have to do.

I call Jacob and to my surprise, Samantha answers his cell phone. "Uh, Sam, I need your and Jacob's help."

I explain my idea and she laughs at me, "You're fucking crazy boss, but yeah we will help you with whatever you need."

"So, you're gonna tell me why you're answering Jacob's phone?" I ask, with a shit-eating grin on my face, I knew they were into each other.

"That's none of your fucking business, Beaufort Williams." Samantha retorted, and I laughed as she hung up on me.

Did she think they would get by sneaking around without people finding out? I shrug my shoulders and get my truck keys. I have to go into the shop today and then work the bar at the saloon tonight, hopefully, Remmy will show up. If not, Samantha will have to go get her and drag her to the saloon.

THE SALOON IS PACKED when I see Samantha dragging in a reluctant Remington Parker up to the bar. Her eyebrows are raised and a scowl is on her face, her lips are puffed out in a pout and I can't help but to smile at her. She is hating every second of this and I'm sure Samantha will be asking for a raise, she deserves one after putting up with me all these years.

I turn to look at Cletus, a regular who has agreed to help me with what I am about to do. Cletus is a veteran, about sixty-seven years old, and a wildcat, ready for anything. The old man downs his beer and stands up, stumbling over to where Jacob is standing by the bull pit. Butterflies are going crazy in my stomach and I am nervous. I need Remington to talk to me, there's so much we need to work through.

Samantha parks Remmy at the bar and then goes behind it and makes her a drink. When she's finished, she finds me and pats me on the shoulder. "Okay, boss. She promised she would stay until her drink was done. You had better get started."

I inhale deeply and blow it out as I pick up the microphone, the music lowers and everyone starts to quiet. "I made some mistakes lately and I am truly sorry for those who were hurt by my actions. I know that this doesn't make things even, but I hope it makes it better."

The lights overhead dim, as the room is exploding with lights of different colors, I clear the bar as the song "Pony" by Ginuwine comes through the speakers. Jumping up on the wood surface, I begin to dance, and slowly unbutton my shirt. The crowd goes wild as I grind my hips and shake my ass. I look over at Remmy and a stern look is on her face as if she's unfazed by my act. I slide down on my stomach and dig my hips into the bar thrusting as if I was having sex. I then jump back up, turn and jump off the bar making my way to the bullpit where Jacob helped Cletus up and he is waiting for me. I nod at Jacob and he starts the mechanical bull, it's moving slowly and starting to circle. I leap on behind Cletus and pull him close to me. The crowd goes wild with hollering and laughter as I hold Cletus's arm and we move in unison on the cow, almost like we are lovers. I push him forward, smacking him on his ass. And pull him back up. I then scoot backwards so I can stand up and move in front of him. The old man is laughing, having a fun time, obviously enjoying the attention and the atmosphere. Not giving a fuck about what people think, he grabs my butt and pulls me down to face him. He wraps his withered arms around my head and leans in close.

"You better make things right with your girl," he whispers, before he pulls my face to his and kisses me hard on the mouth.

The whole saloon goes nuts, some laughing, some yelling, some I'm sure in shock. As he pulls away, I laugh because the kiss was not part of the routine, I hug the old man and jump off the bull, waiting for it to stop completely before helping him off.

"Thanks for the ride, I figured I would try it one time before I die," he says, as he makes his way over to where Jacob is, to put his shoes back on.

The music and lights go back to normal and everything is as they were before Cletus and my sexy show. I look at the bar and realize Remington is no longer sitting there. I scurry up to Samantha and she hands me a slip of paper. It has my name written on the outside. I unfold it and read:

Beaufort, Your show with Cletus was a start. You're right we do need to talk. Meet me after closing, where we shared our first kiss. P.s. Am I going to make Cletus jealous? P.s.s. He isn't another friend-with- benefits is he?

Yours, Remmy

I laugh as I fold the note backup and stuff it into my pocket. Hopefully, I will get the answers I've needed for the last ten years and get my girl back.

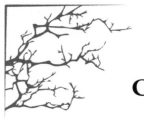

Chapter Twenty

Remington

I got to say answering the door and finding the sarcastically bubbly Samantha standing on the other side was a surprise. She was dressed in her work uniform and was looking antsy, moving her hands animatedly. She practically gets on her hands and knees and begs me to follow her to the saloon.

"Why? Bubba doesn't need me there. Y'all do well without me." I reach out to help her off the ground.

"Please, I swear you don't have to stay long. One drink and you can leave." She has her hands folded in front of her as if she's praying.

"One. Just one drink and I am gone." I snatch my wallet and keys from the table and follow Samantha out to the driveway and slide into my vehicle.

"I'll follow you," she shouts, as she starts her car and I pull out headed to Blue Moon.

I know something is going to go down and the thought of it has my guts bubbling and nerves rack my body. I swallow them down. Just one drink. I think as I climb out and meet Samantha to walk into the saloon. The bar is busy, the parking lot full of vehicles of every shape and color scattered around. We are open Thursday through Saturday, six p.m. until one a.m. and every night we open we always have a crowd at least that is what I've noticed since being back in Jackson.

"One drink Sam, I mean it," I say, as I sling open the door and head straight for a vacant bar stool and she moves behind the counter to make me a Jack and Coke. I see my favorite purple-headed bartender chat with Bubba and he grabs the microphone and starts giving out an apology like he's Oprah Winfrey giving out cars. I roll my eyes dramatically and sip my drink. It's going to take more than that to earn my forgiveness.

The music starts up and I realized it's the song from the movie, Magic Mike and when Bubba jumps onto the bar and starts stripping I couldn't believe my eyes. His muscular, athletic body shaking and moving to the rhythm has my panties wet and I curse myself for being so weak. I swear I about orgasm as I watch him grind his crotch into the wood wishing, like the rest of the women in the bar I'm sure, that I was the wood or at least beneath his magnificent body. I try to show no emotion as I see him turn his gaze on me before he climbs down and saunters over to the bullpit. Where an old man, they call Cletus, is sitting on the bull, his skinny frame holding on to the leather strip just behind the fake bull's head.

Bubba jumps on the back of the mechanical bull and I am stunned. He is doing the same movements with Cletus he did with the blonde. I can't help but to laugh at the scene in front of me. The whole saloon is going wild, laughing and yelling and cheering them on as the old man pulls Bubba in and kisses him. Ok. That might be a start to a little forgiveness. I pull out a scrap of paper from my wallet and ask Sam for a pen as I jot down a note for Bubba. I leave a tip under my glass and give Samantha the note.

It's time to tell Bubba everything, time to come clean about the past. This will either make us or break us.

Chapter Twenty-One

Bubba

"If you don't work here or fuck with someone who works here, it's time to pay your tabs, give me a twenty percent tip and head on out. It's last call, y'all!" Samantha says, on the microphone before drunk patrons mosey up to the register or put wads of cash on their tables for the buckle bunnies to pick up for their tabs. The music stops and we all start cleaning up after locking up the door behind the last customer.

"You should really go meet Remmy," Samantha says, as I pass her to restock the bar of liquor. "I will make sure everything is cleaned up and locked up before I leave."

I lean forward and kiss Samantha on the cheek. "You're the best, you know that right?"

"Of course," she says, wiping off the kiss as if she might get cooties. "Go get your girl, Boss."

There's a slight chill in the air as I make my way to my truck. I open the door and slip inside, pulling out the note that Remmy wrote me. Our first kiss, damn that was so long ago but I can remember it like yesterday.

The crowd is going wild, the smell of dirt, sweat and perfume hits my nostrils as I take Remmy into my arms. The Bobcats won their first game of the season and Remmy ran to congratulate me.

"You did so good Bubba, I'm proud of you," she squeals as she jumps into my arms and I swing her around.

"Thank you, Rem." Her face moves closer to mine as I bend towards her. Our lips collide in a sweet, slow kiss.

I still can remember the tastes of her strawberry lip gloss and hear the moan that escaped her lips before our kiss ended. That was the day I knew I'd love Remington Parker the rest of my life. I put the note back into my pocket and started the engine. Nerves invade me, but I quickly push them away. We need this. I need this. I need to know what made my girl run from me all those years ago, knowing that no matter what I will not lose her again.

The drive to the High School football field is short. There is only one vehicle in the lot. I pull in beside her and turn the truck off, pulling out my keys and putting them in my pocket. I inhale deeply and blow out. I can absolutely do this.

I step out of my truck and look towards the field, standing in the exact spot is my girl, wearing a dress similar to the one she was wearing the day we first kissed. Beautiful. I walk to her and she turns around a small smile on her face.

Chapter Twenty-Two

Remington

Butterflies flutter in my stomach as I hear Bubba's truck pull into the school's parking lot. The smell of freshly mowed grass is in the air, crickets are chirping and lightning bugs are dancing through the sky. I know this conversation is a long time overdue and that I've kept this secret from him for long enough. I know that he deserves the absolute truth on why I left so abruptly so many years ago and why it took my father's death to bring me back to this small little town in Kentucky. Gathering my strength and curbing my nerves, I turn around to look at the man that stole my heart so many years ago.

I look him over, the tight denim jeans that fit his athletic figure so well, the way his shirt clings to his broad muscular chest, the thickness of the arms that use to hold me tight. He hasn't changed much in the last ten years, the facial hair is filled in and longer, his hair is now grown out and hits his shoulders. He was a good-looking boy, but the man standing before me was nothing short of gorgeous. I can tell from the way he is walking and his facial expressions he has no idea about what he is about to hear and he is as nervous as I am. I'm not sure if that's a good or bad thing, but we will find out. When he finally reaches me, I grab him by the hand and lead him to the bleacher stands and sit down.

"I want to say I'm sorry for not telling you about Arlene. She has always been a good friend to me. It was a shitty thing for me to not tell you and for me to keep that I was seeing you from her." He looks down and waits for my response.

"It's ok Bubba. I'm over it and I talked to Arlene yesterday. She is working through things. She is going to be okay too." A look of relief washes over his face and he shakes his head.

"I guess I should start on why I asked you to meet me here tonight." I take a deep breath and slowly release it. "There was a lot about me I kept from you back then. I had to. I hated keeping secrets from you, but it was the only way I could survive."

"Survive?" He looks at me questionably. "What do you mean, Remmy?"

"Let me start from the beginning, then you will understand." I pat his leg and he shakes his head as I open my mouth to tell him about the darkness that has haunted me my whole life and the secrets I have kept hidden for a decade.

"My mother passed away when I was born. I never had a mom and my dad started drinking shortly afterwards. Everyone knew he was a drunk, but by some miracle I survived his neglect and I'm pretty sure it was from helping his "lady friends." After I got older everything I did would make him upset. He would yell at me, put me down, tell me he wished I would have died, that I took her away from him. I was miserable, I remember sitting in my bedroom being as quiet as I could sobbing, wondering why my father didn't love me like kids at schools. As I grew older, the abuse got worse. He would hit me with belts, punch me, smack me, make me kneel on grains of rice on the floor for hours until my knees would bleed. I had no one else, no one to tell, nowhere to go. When dad got the job on the horse farm and we moved here, I thought things were going to be different, but I was wrong. So, very fucking wrong. I was fourteen the first time he came into my room and touched me. He would call me by my mother's name and I could always smell the alcohol on his breath. I was scared of him, scared to tell, scared to say anything. I laid there willing my mind to go anywhere else, disassociating with the horrible things my father was doing to me. He would finish and then leave and the next morning it was like it didn't happen. He was the same old, cantankerous man he always was. It started off slow only once or twice every few months, but the more my body grew and matured the more frequently it happened. His violent outburst became more frequent as well."

I wipe the tear that has leaked from my eye as Bubba pulls me into his gigantic arms. "Tell me baby girl, lean on me. Give me all your pain," he whispers into my ear, as I lay my head on his shoulders.

"After you and I started dating, I could leave the house and it wasn't as bad. He stopped coming to my room at night and I never had to listen to his hateful words. Do you remember the night of the bonfire? The one after y'all beat Perry and we all celebrated out at the Smith's?" I look up at him and he shook his head yes and I continued my story. "I was late getting home. Dad was three sheets to the wind and in a foul mood. His and my mother's wedding photo in his lap, old music flowing from the radio and I knew what was about to come. I could see it in his face when he looked at me. I felt nothing but terror. I couldn't, no I wouldn't let him touch me again. Not if I could help it, not after just giving my heart, soul and body to you. He was too strong though, the more I fought him, the more he enjoyed it. It was like a game to him and when he ripped my panties from me, I begged him to stop, I screamed at him. "Daddy, please don't hurt me." But, my dad wasn't there, only a monster."

Tears tracked down my face, I was full on sobbing now. Bubba was holding me tight, wiping my tears and just held me until I was ready to continue. He was quiet, that unnerved me, because I had no inclination of what he was thinking.

"After he situated himself in me, I went blank. I couldn't move. I couldn't do anything, but lay there. It was as if I was in a nightmare I couldn't wake from. When he finished he got up, righted himself and went back to his bedroom. I showered in the hottest water, scalding myself and scrubbing my skin trying to get rid of the feeling of him on me, but it never went away. The feeling of disgust and hatred filled me.

For the next few months, he didn't look at me, didn't speak a word. I tried to act normal at school and around you. I was embarrassed, scared that you would hate me or blame me and I couldn't deal with that. Then I started gaining weight, staying sick, and always tired. I thought I was getting the flu or something. It was the day of graduation, when I got home, my father shoved a pregnancy test at me and watched as I went into the bathroom and peed on it. He stood over me and when the two pink lines showed up saying I was pregnant, I knew I had to leave. I wasn't going to let my child live through the hell I have. When he looked at the test and saw the results he called me names and beat me so bad I could barely walk. The next morning, before he woke up I left on a bus to Ohio. The only money I had was what I was saving from cleaning Miss Napier's house and from babysitting. I packed my clothes and a few things that meant something to me and I left Jackson Kentucky, my father, and you."

Chapter Twenty-Three

Bubba

Shock. That's what I'm feeling, and total and utter confusion. Why? Why did she not tell me she was living in pure hell, the unmistakable pain she endured just being in the house with the man that caused her to suffer. One of the people that you're supposed to be able to trust, that's supposed to love you unconditionally, that's supposed to protect you made her life unbearable. I gather her in my arms and hold her tightly, holding her so close it was as if I lightened my grip on her. She might run away and I couldn't allow that. Not again. Never again was I going to lose her. I have so many questions, I think back and try to remember signs, some kind of "tell" that this was going on. I remember certain times her not wanting me to touch her, or her saying she fell and hurt herself, but no time in my innocent adolescent mind could I have thought that the girl I loved was going through pure agony. I was such a blind fool.

"You think I'm disgusting don't you?" She asks as she looks me in the eyes.

"No baby, never," I state, and it's true. She was a child and didn't know what to do, or how she could get out of the situation. "You are a survivor, you're strong, resilient and fucking amazing Remington."

I move the hair from her face and kiss her lightly on the lips. "I have lots of questions, but I want you to finish. I mean if you want. I want to know what happened when you left Kentucky."

My girl nods her head and takes a deep breath before blowing it out slowly. She grabs my hand and holds it close to her heart, before she continues her story.

Chapter Twenty-Four

Remington

I wipe my sweaty palms off onto my dress as I lay my head back on Bubba's chest so I can continue. The words almost turn to ash in my mouth because I know that what I have to say next will make his world pivot and spiral out of control .

"Do you remember junior year when I needed help in Algebra? I had a student tutor named Genevieve?" I asked as I looked up into his chocolate eyes. He simply nods his head. "We stayed friends even after she graduated, we would write letters, emails and texted each other often. Genevieve left Kentucky to start Ohio University, that's one of the reasons I applied there, she was insistent about me going there for graphic design. When I called her and told her what had happened, she opened up her small apartment to me with open arms. Other than you, she has been the only person I could even call a friend. Genevieve was my savior, she helped me get a job working at a jewelry boutique a few days after I arrived, I slept on her couch and she helped me find an obstetrician. Despite the beating, my baby survived and was healthy and strong. I continued to work at the boutique, saving as much money as I could, and when school started, I moved into family housing on campus. All of the hard work studying, busting my ass, keeping my grades up throughout highschool let me attend college for free. I didn't have to pay for anything and got so many free meals every week at the school's cafeteria, which saved me money on groceries. I could keep most of my work checks and put them in savings. So, for the first two semesters, before having the baby, I worked at the jewelry boutique and during the times I wasn't in classes, I got to remain in the dorm because I worked helping a professor as his personal assistant. I gave birth in March to a healthy beautiful baby girl named Penelope. She has been my life, my whole fucking world since the day she was born. Penelope is the reason I survived. I finished college, started a design business, designing websites, book covers and merchandise for authors. I was able to buy a modest home for Penelope and myself and with Genevieve by my side to help I made a successful business and made sure Penelope has everything she wants or could ever need."

"You have a kid?" Bubba says, as he holds me tighter against him.

I pull my head from his shoulder and face him. "Yes, I do Bubba, but that's not everything. "

He moves my head back to his chest. "Okay, tell me everything."

"Penelope could be your daughter. I never had a DNA test because I couldn't handle the fact she could be his," I say, the word his coming out as a hiss. "In my mind, no matter what, Penelope was our daughter. Yours and mine and I wasn't going to let something like genetics take that away from me."

I could feel the second he understood the words coming from my mouth, he tightened beneath me and went rock solid.

"I could be a father?" He whispers, shaking his head as if he is shaking the thought from his mind. "She would be almost eleven years old? "

"Yes, do you want to see her? I have pictures on my phone," I ask, as I scroll to her pictures and hold my phone up so he can see her.

"Remington." My name escapes his lips as he reaches for my phone.

The picture is of Penelope wearing a purple dress, her long brownish-red hair in pigtails and a smile across her beautiful freckled face.

"She looks like you with brown hair!" He exclaims, holding the phone closer to his face scrutinizing the picture. "Her eyes are green like yours."

"If you want to take a DNA test Bubba we can arrange it." Is the only words I can manage to say as he flips through the pictures on my cell. Each one of Penelope or us both through the years.

"Remington Parker, can you not look at her and see?" He takes my face into his hand and forces me to look at him, "That is MY daughter. She has my nose, my mother's hair, look." He points at a side picture of Penelope coloring. "Those are my fucking ears Rem. Mine. She is my daughter. I don't need any fucking test to tell me that."

"So..so..you're not mad?" I whimper. "I know it's a lot to deal with."

"Mad?! Why would I be mad? I'm a daddy!" He pulls me off his lap, stands up, and runs his fingers through his hair and starts pacing. "Rem, I've got to meet her."

"You can do that. I'll arrange for Genevieve to bring her here." I wrap my arms around myself happy in the fact that my secrets are out and I am finally free of the guilt and embarrassment that has weighed me down for years.

Maybe, just maybe we can make this work and be the family I've always dreamed about.

Chapter Twenty-Five

Bubba

A dad. I'm a fucking dad. I have a ten year old daughter. I can't believe it. I stare at the little girl. She can't be but about six months old in the picture, she's sleeping, a light frosting of hair on her head, so unbelievably adorable. My daughter. I know in my heart and soul she's mine. I trace the picture with my finger. She reminds me of my mother, she has the same nose my mother blessed me with and the ears passed down from my father. Yes, definitely my daughter. I stop pacing long enough to hand Remmy back her phone.

"Please, send me all those pictures. Tell me about her. Tell me about Penelope! What's her middle name? Does she like school? What's her likes and dislikes?" I shoot questions at her like I'm at a verbal shooting range.

Remmy explodes into laughter and I can't turn off the smile from my face. "Her middle name is Adelia. My mom's name. She absolutely loves school and she is very smart."

"Are you going to tell her I'm her father?" My eyebrows shoot up as I anticipate the answer.

"She already considers you her father. I use to tell her stories about us all the time. Her bedside table has a picture of us together at prom. It's getting late Bubba, do you think we should go home and you digest all this information. I mean you never questioned anything? You should really think about all this before I have Genevieve bring her down here to meet you."

"There's nothing to think about Remington. She is my daughter, I want to meet her and spend time with her. That's that. It is late though, come on I will walk you to your car, unless you want to come to my place for the night." I smirk at her and I can tell she was thinking about it.

"I think it's best for us to go our separate ways for the night. We can talk more tomorrow." She stands up and takes my hand in hers as we walk back through the stands to the parking lot where our vehicles wait.

I open the car door for her and she kisses my cheek before getting in. "Thank you for being so understanding."

"You don't have to thank me, Remington. I'm just glad I know the truth now. I thought the reason why you left was because we had sex the night before. I thought maybe you felt pressured or that you didn't want me anymore." Remington peers up at me with a look of sadness on her face.

"Bubba, that night was one of the best nights of my life. You didn't pressure me into anything. I wanted you, I wanted everything we did that night. I am sorry I made you feel that way." Remmy leans forward and kisses me softly on the lips.

"It's okay Rem. Thank you for finally telling me the truth." I gently touch her face, place a kiss on her forehead and step away from her vehicle. "Be safe on your way home."

I CHECK THE TIME AND realize it's almost 3:30. Damn, maybe I need to head home too. I climb into my truck with thoughts of an adorable ten year old and her mother run through my mind. Mine. Not just my daughter, but Remington too. They are mine and I'm not letting either one leave me.

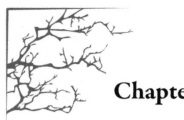

Chapter Twenty-Six

Remington

"All Your'n" by Tyler Childers is blasting from my phone. I rake my hand over the bed and clasp my phone hitting the green button. "Hello." My voice is gravely and filled with sleep.

"Mama!" The cutest voice comes over the phone. I sit up and look at the time. 9:35.

"Hi, baby girl. Are you having fun with Auntie G?" I clear my throat and make my way to the bathroom, hitting the mute button as I relieve my bladder.

"Of course, but mama we miss you. When are you coming home?" Her voice has turned whiney and sad and it truly breaks my heart.

"I was thinking about asking Aunt Genevieve if she will bring you here for the weekend. Would you like that?" I wipe myself and flush the toilet, making my way to the sink to wash my hands.

"Heck yeah!" She has the phone away talking in the background saying please oh please can we, when I hear her hand the phone over.

"Remmy?" Genevieve states my name as if it's a question.

"G. Would you want to come down and bring Penelope? You can stay here with me and check out the saloon. I take a breath and whisper, "and meet Bubba."

"Umm, is there something I should know?" Genevieve questions, but she should already know the answer.

"I told Bubba everything last night and he wants to meet Pen. I think it would be good for both of them. Please come, I miss you both." I put toothpaste on a toothbrush and start brushing my teeth.

"Of course Remmy, we will come Friday. I need to meet Prince Charming, officially. I mean of course I knew of him in high school, but we never met."

"Don't tell Penelope. I want to surprise her," I say before hanging up. "Talk to you later, give Pen a kiss for me. Love you like a sister from a different mister.``

I rinse my mouth out and run a brush through my hair. Good enough for today. I pull up Bubba's name and type him one word, Friday. I hope he's ready for reality to smack him in the face. Cause it's coming at him fast like a bullet.

After choosing my clothes for today, a black tank top and a pair of jeans I check my phone to see if Bubba has text back. He hasn't. Maybe he's changed his mind after thinking about our discussion and decided against meeting Penelope. Maybe he wants a DNA test after all. I don't know, but him not texting back for hours has me anxious and I don't love the feeling. I put on my sandals and fetch my keys. I'm hungry and Olivia's Diner has the best breakfast in all of Kentucky. Just thinking about the homemade biscuits and gravy has my mouth watering.

The diner is small and cozy, the tables are full all besides one in the back and I make my way to it. I see Arlene heading towards me and I'm glad to see that she's looking good. Her hair has been cut to her shoulders and she's in an old band t-shirt and jeans. That girl could make a potato sack look sexy I believe.

"Come sit with me," I say, over the high frequency of the people chatting. "I'm alone and starving."

A smile crosses her pale face as she pulls a sit out and plops in it. "I always stop in here for a doughnut and coffee."

"Oliva's is the best for breakfast for sure." I agree looking over the menu even though I know exactly what I'm going to order. "So, how are you doing?"

"Thank you, I was hoping we wouldn't have to drag out the pleasantries for long. I am doing much better. I got hung up on expectations and was blind for a minute, that's all. I knew Bubba wasn't for me, but it stung a little and I guess my ego got deflated."

She sits back into her chair and takes a deep breath. "How are you?"

"Good for you. A queen always knows her worth and you will find the perfect guy for you soon, I'm sure. I am doing good, really good and I feel like my life is heading in a good direction." I won't go into detail about my situation because Arlene seems friendly, but I don't know her enough to spill my guts.

An old woman in a waitress uniform comes up with a pen in her hair and a pen and paper in her hands, "What can I get you gals?" Her voice is hoarse probably from years of smoking.

"I will take my regular, Linda," Arlene says, as she hands her the menu.

"I want gravy and biscuits, sausage, a coffee with cream and sugar and a Coke. Thank you, Linda." I also handed her my menu.

"You should come to the saloon tonight. We are having ladies night. First drink free. The rest are half off. It would be good to hang out and I know Bubba would love to see you. He's been worried about losing his best friend." I look into her pretty hazel eyes. "I'm serious. He misses you."

"I will think about it, Remmy. I don't know," she says, crossing her arms in a defense move.

"No worries. It was just a suggestion." I hold up my hands. "You can do whatever you want to do."

"Okay damn. I'll come, you never know I might find the love of my life there tonight," she says, as Linda brings us our drinks and Arlene takes a gulp of her coffee.

"Nectar from the God's!" Arlene says, as she takes another sip and then laughs.

"I really want us to be friends, I need some good friends around here. I mean if there's no hard feelings about Bubba," I say, drinking my Coke.

"No hard feelings at all, Remmy." We are served our breakfast and continue small talk and eventually she has to leave for work. We say our goodbyes and I truly hope to see her in the saloon tonight.

Chapter Twenty-Seven

Bubba

A new day. New possibilities and a shit ton of things I need to put into action to keep my girls here in Jackson with me. I sniff my pits, first though I need a shower. I climb out of bed, the sheets falling from my naked body and trot to the bathroom, my bladder is going to bust. After I'm done, I turn on the shower to hot and wait for it to heat up. When it's just the way I want it, I climb inside the warm water engrossing me and relaxing my muscles. Nothing beats a hot shower. Well, a few things do like the feel of Remmy's lips on mine and a homemade pecan pie. So, a hot shower is like a third, okay. Sex is definitely number two. I run the shampoo through my hair, the smell of citrus filling the air making me rejuvenated. I lather up and rinse off, turning off the water. I grab a towel and wrap it around me as I walk up to the bathroom mirror. I need to shave and take care of my beard, but first my teeth need to be brushed.

After getting my teeth clean, I trim my beard, shave the access and apply some beard oil, brushing it out with my beard comb. I also comb out my hair. Then admire myself in the mirror.

"Looking good today, Bubba, " I say, to myself as I walk out of the bathroom and into my closet.

I dig into my closet and find a red and black plaid shirt to wear over a white shirt and a pair of jeans. I put them on, grab a belt and slip on my socks and shit kickers. I spray my cologne on and pick up my phone where I see Remmy has messaged me.

Me: Friday is good. What are you doing today?

Remmy: I just had breakfast with Arlene. She might come to ladies night tonight.

Me: I hope she does. We need to talk. I want to see you.

Remmy: Yes, you need to work things out with her. You want to meet me somewhere?

Me: How about you come to my house around 2?

Remmy: Okay Beaufort. See you at 2.

Me: Be thinking about you until then, Remington.

Remmy: My name is Remmy.

I chortle because she has always hated the fact her dad named her after a gun. I slip my phone into my pocket and grab my house keys as I make my way out the door. I have supplies I need and things to buy.

I STOP BY THE GROCERY store's deli and get sandwich meat and cheeses, grapes, olives, and other foods for the picnic I have planned. I also get wine and beer, which I'm sure Remmy is more a beer gal than wine, but things change. I stop by the florist and get a dozen mixed flowers and head back home to get the libations ready for our lunch. When that's finished, I go outside, the air is warm and it's a beautiful sunny day. I check the boat and fill up the tank on the motor. I put a blanket on the bench inside and once I'm sure it's ready for the water, I go inside for a shower and to get ready for our lunch date. I really hope Remmy likes the surprise picnic on the lake. There's something I want to show her and I think she will love it.

Chapter Twenty-Eight

Remington

I arrive back home and a paper is taped to my door. It's a letter from Derrick Higgins, the guy who has painted the house.

Miss Parker,

We are finished with the painting. If you see anything that isn't up to par let us know. Thank you for your payment. It's paid in full.

-D. Higgins

I didn't pay them, there must be some kind of mistake. I think as I open the door and step in, I lay the paper on the entryway table and go upstairs. I open my closet and sift through my clothes. I need something cute, but I can wear it no matter what he has in mind for me. I picked out a cute off the shoulder blouse and a pair of tight dark denim jeans. I can wear a cute pair of sandals or sneakers and of course my new lace bra and panties set. I lay my clothes on the bed before I go to shower.

I grab a razor out of the cabinet as I step into the shower. The water takes a few minutes before it heats up, when it does I stand underneath the waterfall and let it soothe me. The warmth relaxes my muscles and brings calmness to me. I take the lavender shampoo and put a glob in my hand rubbing it into my hair, my fingers working it thoroughly in my scalp. I rinse and conditioner then wash off with some new body wash I picked up at the store. Once I'm done, I shave my legs and underarms, and debate whether or not I should shave my pussy. I mean am I ready to sleep with Bubba? Does he want to? This is a big decision, I mean if I don't shave that means I will not have sex with him, if I do and the chance happens I will definitely jump at the chance. I pick up the shaving cream and put it all over my no-no square and run the razor through it. Too late to stop now, I think as I finish my grooming and wash the pubes and foam down the drain. Sex is definitely on the table today.

Wrapping a fuzzy towel around me, I step out of the shower, and look in the mirror. Time to brush my teeth and get ready for tonight. Forty minutes later, I am dressed, light make-up on, hair up in a ponytail, and ready for the date.

Is it a date? I think it is. I call Penelope and talk to her for a few minutes before I drive to Bubba's house arriving a few minutes early. I take a deep breath and climb out of the vehicle, glad I chose sneakers instead of sandals as I make my way to the front door of his house. His house is beautiful, old-timey with large windows and painted Grey and blue. There's a wrap around porch and a porch swing and. Different plants and flowers are everywhere. Something you wouldn't think a bachelor would care about. When I step on the porch, Bubba opens the door and I can't believe my eyes. He is sexy as hell, wearing a blue button down and slacks, his long auburn hair to his shoulders and his beard trimmed well. I wipe my mouth because I'm pretty sure I'm drooling before swaying closer to him. He embraces me in a hug and kisses my forehead. His cologne fills my nostrils with his manly scent and I could stand here in his arms all day.

"I'm taking you out on the lake, I prepared a picnic." He grabs my hand and we walk around the house on the porch to the back yard where there is a little path to the lake.

"It's so beautiful here. The house is really nice Bubba. You've done pretty good for yourself." Instead of replying he grabs my hand and pulls me through the path.

Chapter Twenty-Nine

Bubba

I help Remmy climb into the dinghy. The small white tin boat rocks gently as she sits down on the middle bench and I cross over into it to join her. The basket of things I prepared is already In the boat. I brought them out earlier, when I was preparing for our date and I pulled the string on the motor to start it.

"I have never done this." She screams over the noise of the boat, her hands turning white as she holds on tight to the sides of the boat.

"Hold on, try to stay balanced, don't lean to one side, if you do it could tip over and we both will end up in the lake," I say, pulling the handle and navigating the boat towards where I want to go.

After a few minutes, she calms down, removing the death grip on the boat and folds her hands onto her lap. She looks around and is checking everything out around us. The lake is beautiful and so clear you can see fish swimming in it. I smile when I notice her sticking her hand in the water and I hit a setting on the motor to make us go a little faster. Once we get to the middle of the lake, I turn off the motor and sit down opposite of Remmy facing her.

"Are you hungry?" I say, taking out the bottle of wine and using the opener to pop the cork filling her wine glass full. I hand it to her and start getting out the sandwiches. "I've made sandwiches, and a pecan pie for dessert."

"You made a pecan pie?" She raises an eyebrow in question. "You might have bought one, but I don't think you can bake."

"Okay, I bought the pie. I did make the sandwiches though," I say, with a smirk as I pass her a sandwich. "I definitely can bake a pecan pie though."

"You shouldn't start our relationship out with a lie," she says, before biting off a corner of the sandwich.

"We're in a relationship?" I say, taking a bite of my own. "Okay, I try to bake. I can warm things up in the oven very well. That better?"

"Yes. To both of those questions." She takes a gulp of the wine.

"Good to know."

I watch as she places her bitten sandwich to the side and slips forward towards me. The boat begins to rock gently with her movements.

"What are you doing, Remmy?" I ask, placing my sandwich to the side as I help her move towards me.

"I'm going to kiss you." She lunges forward causing the boat to lean to the left.

"Sit back down. I will come to you." I wait until she's seated back on her bench and I move to her.

I kneel in front of her and lean forward, brushing her hair from her face, I tilt my head towards hers as I wrap my hand around her head. Our lips collide and it's as heavenly as I remember it being. Our lips crash together as if we are each other's life force. Our tongues invading each other's mouths, a moan escapes as I pull her closer to me deepening the kiss. My free hand roams to the edge of her shirt as I slip it under, caressing the skin underneath. I make my way to her bra and rub her nipple with my thumb.

"Is this okay?" I murmur.

"Yes," She manages to say as she pulls back and takes off her shirt and brings me back to her.

I glide my hand back to her bra and unlatch it, before bringing my hand back cupping and feeling her large breast in my hand. I move away from her lips, kissing and nipping my way down her neck, pulling her bra completely off in the process. I admire her beauty for a second before I wrap my mouth around her nipple, sucking it into my mouth, flicking my tongue over the bud. My other hand massages the other and I know when Remmy takes my hand and moves it between her legs that she is wanting me as much as I want her. Her hands move under my shirt gripping me to her and she whispers in my ear, "fuck me."

I pull my mouth from her and go to her pants unbuttoning them, as she moves her hip to help me slide her pants off the movement causes the boat to rock. I'm so in the zone I notice that when I try removing her tight pants from her legs the boat leans to the right and as I try to balance us I over correct sending the boat and us into the water.

I swim to grab Remmy and hold her to me as I turn the boat right side up. A shocked look comes over her as I place her back inside. Her jeans now really heavy and tight with water hang half way off of her and she struggles with taking them the rest of the way off. I swim to savage what I can and climb back into the dinghy.

"Well that didn't go as planned." I look at my girl and she has a smile on her face.

"I don't know, I think this was your plan. Get me out here, get me turned on, then throw me in the water," She says, as she wrings out her jeans. Now sitting in just her black lace thongs.

I lick my lips."Let me get you back to my house and I will make it up to you."

"I think you better plan on making it up to me more than once." She then starts to laugh as I start the motor and get us back to my home.

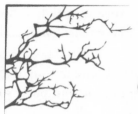

Chapter Thirty

Remington

A chill comes over me and I wrap my arms around me to stave it off. Here I am sitting on this rickety fishing boat in nothing but a black thong, my hair is a mess and I imagine looking like a drowned rat. We arrive at the dock a lot quicker than it took to get to where we were and Bubba ties the boat and climbs out holding his hand out to me. I clasp his hand as I pull myself up and I crash into him causing him to lose his balance. He falls back and pulls me on top of him.

I straddle him, his clothes are wet as I try to pull his shirt up, he helps me as he lifts up and pulls it over his head. We are a wet mess, but I don't care as I make my way to his pants.

"Want to continue what we started?" I ask, as I undo his belt, waiting for an answer.

He flips me over, moving his wet tshirt beneath me and finishes unbuttoning his jeans. Moving them down. "I don't have condoms out here. If you want me to carry you to the house, we can finish there."

"I'm clean Bubba and I'm on birth control," I reply, by pushing his jeans lower.

"I've only been with Arlene," he states, and I know by the way her heart was broken she probably hadn't slept with anyone else but Bubba, so he was probably clean too.

He tears my panties off as his lips make their way back to mine. Kissing me with the heat of a burning sun, he bites my bottom lip causing it to dribble blood. I moan at the sensation as he sucks the blood from my lip. I like knowing that there's a part of me in him now, that forever, a part of me will always be with him. His hands are roaming my body and I feel his huge erection against my thigh as his hand makes its way down my body. His fingers enter my slick pussy and I tighten around his fingers.

"God, you feel so good," He moans, his thumb circling my clit, causing me to buck my hips closer to him. "I want to eat your pussy so bad baby, and I will later, but right now I need to be inside of you."

He removes his hand from me, and I feel him rubbing his cock through my slit, and all at once he thrusts inside of me to the hilt. The intrusion causes me to tighten my legs around him and a groan escapes me. I bite into his shoulder as he begins impelling me faster and harder, the feeling overcomes me as his hand once again slips between us and he pinches my clit between his fingers causing me to climax and I scream as my fingernails dig into his back and I have never came so hard in my whole God damn life. He soon chases his release, as he pulls out of me he sprays his come all over my chest and stomach, marking me as he braces himself over me, kissing my forehead and rolling to the side.

Nothing but heavy breathing can be heard for a few moments, then he sits up, climbing to a stand and pulls Me up taking me into his muscular arms. "Let's go get a shower, I'll give you something of mine to wear."

I hold on tightly as he makes his way to his home through the path and my head nestles into his neck. Tired and blissfully satisfied, I sigh as he carries me through his house into his bathroom where he places me on the sink. He sets the shower water and then grabs my hips, pulling me to him and places a sweet jest kiss on my lips and maneuvers me into the shower.

Chapter Thirty-One

Bubba

I lather the shampoo into Remmy's hair and run my fingers through it. It's all tangled from the lake and our fucking on the dock. The mewling noise that comes from her as I massage her head sends a bolt to my cock, making me hard. God, the noises she makes. I rinse her hair and lather up my hands with soap as I run my hands all over body, making sure every inch of her is clean before finally adding the conditioner to her hair and working it through.

"Your turn," she says, as I finish rinsing her off and she spins around a devilish grin on her face.

She reaches for the soap and I bend down to make it easier for her to wash my hair but instead her dainty hand wraps around my dick. I moan out her name as she tightens her grip and begins to jack me off. Her hand moves faster and rougher and I begin to buck into it. She moves to let the water hit me before she gets on her knees before me. She kisses the tip, and licks the precum that formed at the head. Her warm mouth takes me in, and I place my hand behind her head pulling me into her deeper. When she gags a little I lighten up, then do it again. Liking the way she sounds choking on my cock. She places one hand at the base and starts bobbing her head, the feeling has me seeing stars behind my eyes. She runs her fingers to my asshole and sticks one in causing me to come. She removes her finger and drinks me down, not spilling a drop. I pull her up to me and attack her mouth.

"That was the best fucking blow job ever!" I say, meaning every fucking word.

"You're welcome." She pulls away from me and winks before heading out of the shower.

I finish my shower and walk into her dressed in my shirt. It's tight on her curvy frame and the sight has me hard again. "Calm the fuck down," I whisper to my cock, before grabbing a white tee shirt from my closet and a pair of jeans.

"You look fucking fantastic in my shirt."

"I know," Remmy replies, as she slides into a pair of my jogging pants. "I'm going to head to my house and get ready for ladies night."

"Okay, baby," I say, moving towards her, giving her a long, deep kiss as she walks out of my bedroom.

I hear her horn blow as she drives off, and already I miss her.

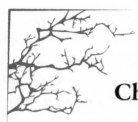

Chapter Thirty-Two

Remington

I strut into the saloon and it is packed, ladies in all shapes sizes and ethnic backgrounds are getting their drink on and in for a fun night. This is the first ladies night that Blue Moon has ever had and it was a suggestion made by Samantha on how to perk up business. The music is booming, ladies are dancing and the fellows are watching closely. I go behind the bar and put on an apron, ready to help Sam out with drinks when Arlene calls my name. I can tell she is already tipsy as she walks my way, swaying a little.

"Hey, you made it!" I scream over the music so she could hear me. Arlene wraps her arms around me and hugs me tight.

"I did and I am having a great night," She says, as she kills the shot in her hand.

"That is awesome, want a refill?" I say, showing her the bottle of Jack Daniels.

"Nah, I think I better take it a little slower, just give me a Coke, please." Arlene flops down beside a rugged guy wearing a leather cut with a bird on it that says Murder of Crows MC on it. I've seen the guys that wear that around sometimes as I was growing up, but I never was around many people who were motorcycle enthusiasts, so I didn't know much about them. I fill Arlene a glass of Coke and sit in front of her.

"You good?" I ask the big, burly guy whose name is Sweets, if the patch on his vest is true.

"Another beer please." He shows me the bottle and I grab him another one, opening it and handing it to him. "Thank you," he says, as he takes a swig of the beer and places it back down,

I jog over to Samantha as she is making a drink for a customer. "Do you know that guy over there with Arlene? I have never seen him before." I try to be nonchalant as I point to the big biker.

"No, I've never seen him. Members of the motorcycle club come in from time to time, they usually drink a beer or two then leave. They have their own biker bar they frequent." She hands the customer his drink and turns to me. "Let her have her fun, she deserves it."

"I am going to, I just don't want her to get hurt again." I nod my head as a customer walks up to the bar wanting five shots.

The night is busy and I haven't had time to check where Bubba might be. I hate to ask Sam, it would seem too much like checking up on him or something. I pick up a tray and make my way through the crowd, grabbing up empty glasses and finishing off bottles of beers, wiping down tables as I go. The music stops and the lights go off and suddenly everyone is thrown into the dark. The whole saloon goes crazy as different colored strobe lights start flashing across the bar and out comes Jacob the bull guy, Bubba and another guy and they start dancing to a slow sultry song. I can't believe my eyes, all the hotness going on and my mouth opens in shock as they all start peeling off their shirts. In front of me are three fine ass looking muscular men. I'm so fucking lucky I think as I watch them finish thier show. The ladies love the dance and go nuts hollering and hooting and cheering the guys on. When the dance is done, he looks up and his eyes are on me, sweat is pouring from his face and his chest is soaked and I swear he looks like he just came from a porn set. He grabs the tray that I am holding and puts it down. He grabs me and pulls me close to me and slams his lips over mine. He lifts me up and I wrap my legs around him, kissing him back heatedly. The taste of mint gum on his breath. We kiss for what seems like a lifetime and when I finally drop my legs down, they are like jelly. He holds me close to him and I kiss his cheek. I love the way his beard feels against my skin. A juxtaposition of rough and yet softness. I run my fingers through it and pull myself away.

"Giving the ladies a show, yeah?" I wink at him so he knows I'm joking and pick up the tray.

"I want you to ride the bull with me, Remmy," Bubba states, and I look over at the line of scantily clad women that's in line. "It's pretty busy over there," I say, nodding toward the bull pit.

"I mean after we close." A mischievous smile covers his face and I nod my head yes, as I walk away making sure to sway knowing he is watching my ass.

Chapter Thirty-Three

Bubba

T he night is slowing down and patrons are leaving. It was a good night and I'm excited to close up and spend some alone time with my girl. She's been giving me "come fuck me eyes" all night and purposely rubbing herself on me all night. My cock has been half-hard this whole time. I look over at the bar and see Arlene with a member of the Murder of Crows Motorcycle club and glad she seems to be having fun and has forgiven me for my stupid actions and I know I can thank Remmy for being a part of that. The Murder of Crows are mostly decent guys and I have known their president Ace almost all of my life. It happens when you live in a small town. I will give him a heads up though to make sure Arlene is treated well at the club and that she's not club pussy. I know the club girls, the "crowettes" as they call them, are treated decently and they choose the lifestyle, but Arlene is a good girl and I want her taken care of.

Samantha gets on the microphone and gives out her last call as customers come up and clear their tabs or have the buckle bunnies get their tabs straight. Ladies' night was a hit and I think that we should have it at least a couple times a month. I look over at Remmy who is sweeping the floor and talking to Corey, one of the new guys and it's obvious he is flirting with her. I can tell she isn't buying into his sexy body or his charms, because she's basically laughing in his face and giving him a hard time. That's my girl, always giving someone shit. After all the customers are gone and the bar looks half way clean I send my workers home, all besides Remmy.

I lock the doors behind Samantha and Jacob as they leave. Tonight, Remmy and I will not be interrupted and I am going to continue to do what I was planning on doing the night Arlene barged in. I'm going to fuck her on the bull. I had Jacob sterilize the bull before going home because I want it nice and clean so I can dirty it all back up.

I turn on "Pillowtalk" by Zayne and start the bull on the lowest setting. Remmy walks up to me and I take her in my arms, she wraps her legs around me and I pack her into the bullpit. I place her on the mechanical bull facing the back end and kiss her lips, while kicking off my boots then my socks. I remove my button up shirt taking my undershirt with it in one fast swoop, leaving my chest exposed, I place a kiss to her lips as I pull hers up over her head. Her focus comes to me as my hands go to my belt and with one tug it comes off and hits the floor. The bull begins to gyrate and she moves her eyes to follow my actions as it spins around. I take my pants off. As she makes her way back around to me I jump on the bull facing her, pulling her closer to me. I kiss her deep and hard as my fingers make my way up her leg under her skirt and realize she isn't wearing any panties

"You aren't wearing any panties. Did you go bare for me?" I growl, in her ear.

"I took them off earlier. I got them soaked thinking about your cock being inside of me." She opens her legs for me and I can see the wetness on her. Remmy leans back and I bend forward, my tongue licking through her slick, wet pussy.

"You taste like magic," I moan, as I grab her ass, pulling her to me, I run my tongue in her, licking and when I reach her clit and suck her into my mouth, she is bucking and moving and the sounds coming from her edges me on as I stick my finger in her opening, and once she adjusts I had another finger fucking her as I suck her off. I feel inside of her vagina for her g-spot, that ridged part inside her that is going to have her seeing stars, and when I massage like I am summoning a genie, for just a few seconds, she grabs my hair and pushes my face into her and I suck harder and just as she is about to come, I bite her clit and this causes her to gush all over my fingers. I remove my fingers from her moving closer to her mouth. She opens it and sucks her come from my fingers. I will be damned if that isn't the hottest fucking thing I have ever seen in my whole entire life.

Remmy sits up and I kiss her hard and deep, as she straddles me, I line my cock up to her pussy and slam her down on me and a groan comes from her and when she begins to ride me I know I have died and gone to heaven. Our kisses get deeper, her arms wrapped around my neck as I help her move up and down on my cock.

"You feel so good baby," I whisper in her ear, and I get a satisfying moan as a response.

My hands grab her ass and I begin thrusting up and into her faster and deeper. I am so close to coming, but I need her to come again for me. I place one of my hands between us and start rubbing her cunt and when I feel her start to tense I pinch her clit and she screams out in post coital bliss and I chase my release right afterwards. Remmy goes limp into my arms and I wrap mine around her and hold her close to me. We are both satisfied and exhausted. I'm definitely keeping her.

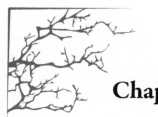

Chapter Thirty-Four

Remington

I hold on tight to Bubba. I really missed him, and having him this close and being this intimate with him, it's almost like the last ten years hasn't happened and we are back in high school. Except we aren't and tomorrow Geniveve and Penelope will be coming and I am nervous about him meeting my daughter. I withdraw myself from his arms and gaze into his eyes, and in that moment I realize that I still love him and always have.

"Are you ready?" I say, moving backwards on the bull, putting distance between us.

"Ready for what?" He asks, as he jumps down and walks to the bull controls and turns it off.

"Ready to meet your daughter?" I say, as I jump off the bull, my knees weak and almost falling onto the mat.

"As I will ever be," he states, as he gathers my clothes and hands them to me and looks around for his. "What if she doesn't like me?"

"Just be yourself, she will adore you Bubba." I say, as I fasten my bra. "She is such a great kid, I mean she really has been so easy to raise. She is smart, funny and really good, she never gets into trouble. I was blessed with such a wonderful child."

"She took after you, of course she's perfect." I sit at a chair and put on my shoes and he sits across from me slipping on his boots.

"You and her will be fine. I promise." I stand up and we walk up front to the bar where I stashed my keys and purse. "They will probably get in early in the morning. I can text you and we can all go out to eat at the diner."

"Sounds good, baby." He tugs me closer and kisses my forehead, both cheeks, my chin then places a chaste kiss on my lips. "Let me get my things and I will walk you to your car."

A few minutes later, we are walking hand and hand into the chilly early morning air. We are both comfortably quiet and just enjoying the moment. When we make it to my vehicle, he grabs the back of my head and kisses me like it is the last time he is going to see me.

"Message me and let me know you made it back home." One more kiss to my forehead and he opens the car door and closes it after I climb in. The engine starts and I watch as he climbs into his truck and I leave the parking lot.

Arriving home a few minutes later, I check my phone and notice a text from Genevieve.

Gen: We are heading out pretty early in the morning. Make sure daddy dearest ain't in the bed with you, don't want Pen to meet her father that way. It might scar her for life.

Me: We haven't got to sleep overs. Yet. So, no worries. I will be home, I will make up the guests room for you and Pen can sleep on the couch. I love you both to the moon and back. Goodnight.

I also sent a text to Bubba telling him that I made it home and was going to sleep. I lock my door and remove my shoes, and go to my bedroom, throwing my clothes in the hamper. Tonight was one of the best nights of my life, the things Bubba can do on that bull is pure enchantment.

I jump in the shower, quickly washing off. Afterwards, I brush my teeth and run a brush through my hair, I grab an old tee shirt and a pair of panties. I climb into the bed and get comfortable, the feeling of being held by Bubba after the best orgasm of my life in my mind as my eyes drift off to sleep.

Chapter Thirty-Five

Bubba

I notice as I pull up to the diner that Remmy's car is parked up front. My hands are sweating, I am having heart palpitations and I swear I am going to vomit all over my nice suit. Yes, I, Beaufort Williams, am wearing a suit to a diner, a small country diner. I take a deep breath and blow it out. I wipe my hands off on my pants and take the key out of the ignition. I step up to the door and Remmy is there to meet me.

"What the hell are you wearing Bubba?" She mutters so low I can barely make out what she is saying.

"I wanted to look nice, first impressions are important." I straighten my tie and clear my throat. "Do you like it?"

"It's perfect if you were going to a wedding or a funeral, not meeting a ten year old little girl in a country diner to eat waffles."

Remmy grabs my hand and pulls me to tables near the back and I spot her and there is no doubt in mind that Penelope is my daughter, she looks just like me when I was her age, minus her long hair.

"Penelope, this is Bubba." Remmy introduces me and I hold my hand out, but she runs into my arms and hugs me instead. I let out a grunt as she grabs a hold of me, not expecting the force.

"I've waited my whole life to meet you." She steps back and looks at me. "You're my dad, right?"

I can't help but admire her straightforwardness. I like the no nonsense approach to this, It makes it easier to deal with and there is no hiding.

"I am," I say, as she grabs my hand and has me sit across from her at the little table.

"My name is Penelope Grace Parker. I'm ten and a half. I like strawberry ice cream. My favorite food is pepperoni pizza. I like to write and I love books," she says, as she takes a bite of waffle.

"She got hungry while we were waiting," Remmy says as she takes a sip of her coffee. "I didn't think you would mind."

"I don't. Of course not. I am Beaufort Allen Williams. I'm 28 and a half years old. I like strawberry ice cream too, but my favorite is pecan pie. My favorite food is ribeye steak and baked potatoes. I like music and dancing, but I do read on occasion too." I flag the server and tell her to give me the same thing Penelope has.

"Are you going to marry my momma?" Penelope takes a drink of her milk eyeing me over the glass.

I look over at Remmy and her face is glowing red. "That is my plan, eventually." Remmy gets choked on her drink and Genevieve laughs.

"Would you want that?" I question her.

"I want momma happy, and if you make her happy, I reckon I am okay with that." She licks whip cream off her spoon and smiles.

"Do you always say what is on your mind?" The server drops off my food and I pour syrup all over my waffles.

"Yep." She takes another bite and smiles with her mouth wrapped around her waffle bite.

"Good to know," I say, as I take a bite of my waffle.

"You remember Genevieve don't you?" Remmy points at her friend, and she does look familiar, but she looks more grown up and not like the meek, mousy girl from high school.

"Of course I do. Hello, Genevieve. It's nice to see you again." I nod my head her way.

"Hello there, Big Daddy, It's good to see you again as well," she says, before she takes a drink of water. "It's been awhile, you're looking good all dressed up in a suit."

"I wanted to look nice." I look down. "Okay, I get it. I am way over dressed."

All three of the ladies bust up laughing and I can't help but to join in. This meeting wasn't as bad or as awkward as I imagined it to be. That eases my thoughts and soon we all are laughing and having a good time.

Chapter Thirty-Six

Remington

"I really like him mom, it's too bad he had to go to work." Penelope climbs into the car and fastens the seatbelt. "Can I call him dad?"

"I am glad that you like him honey, but I think you need to talk to him about what you should call him and maybe no more pressuring him to marry me? He will come over after working at the auto shop." I giggle, as I slip into the driver's side.

"Nonsense. You should lock him in, you should have back then. You have been pining for Bubba for ten years Rem. Sounds like Pen's the wing girl to help you get the job done." Genevieve chuckles, obviously finding the situation amusing.

"No one can resist my cuteness." Penelope pipes in.

"Of course they can't." I shake my head. "Where would you like to go now?"

"Can you drive around and show me the places you liked when you were a kid?" Penelope asks looking out the window watching Bubba get into his truck.

"Can do, baby girl." I say pulling out of the parking lot.

"Mom, I am not a baby." Penelope responds.

"You will always be my baby." I drive to the park that I used to play in when I was about her age.

The park is in better shape now than it was when I was a child. The swings and slides look new and I tell Penelope to go play as Gen and I sit on a bench to talk and where I can keep an eye on her.

"She seems okay with all of this." I peer at Gen who is staring out onto the playground.

"Yes, but are you okay with all of this?" Her eyes meet mine. "This is a lot all at once. Your dad dying, coming clean to Bubba, having them meet. How are you dealing?"

"It is a lot. I think it is all going to be okay. I feel like I am finally on the right path, ya know? I am just confused about what Bubba really wants." I shrug my shoulders. "Knowing you're a father and being a dad are two different things, what if he can't handle being a dad? What if it's too much for him?"

"I think he has taken the news about everything extremely well. I think he is up for the challenge. The thing now is for you to decide if being here, back in this town, living in that house, being with Bubba is what you really want. Do you want to give up everything you have in Ohio, set up your business here, actually be with Bubba again?"

"I know I love him and I don't think I could leave him again Gen. I don't want to have him be a part of Penelope's life then rip them apart. I can't do that to her. Hell, I can't do that to him either."

"Sounds like you have your answer," she says, as she stands up. "Let's go show our girl, what a nap is. I am tired, the drive here has worn me out."

I laugh as I stand up and call Penelope over and we head back to our home. My mind is made up and my heart full.

Chapter Thirty-Seven

Bubba

M e: You and Jacob can handle the saloon tonight right?

Samantha: Of course. Have fun.

Me: Thanks.

Samantha: No problem, Boss man.

I am sitting in my truck. I had to work today at the auto shop, so I had to run home and change out of my suit before work and run after work to shower and decide on my normal clothes for this afternoon. I'm not as nervous as I was this morning and now I have no doubts that my two girls aren't going anywhere. We can live in her house, my house or we can sell them both and buy one together, but she is not leaving me again.

I pick up the flowers I got for my girls and as I am walking in, Gen is walking out.

"Flowers. Good job, Cowboy." She winks, as she passes me.

"Thanks. You're not staying? "

"I think I am going over to Blue Moon, hoping to find a hot date for the night." She smiles.

"We have a new guy named Corey, you might be interested in." I laugh. "The ladies seem to like him."

"Yeah, I'm more interested in the ladies." She winks as she gets into her car.

Well, that's something new. I didn't realize Gen was lesbian; there are a few women that come to the saloon that are lesbian or sexual fluid, so she will more than likely find her a "date." Hell, I know Asa is gay.

"Da...Bubba!" A loud screech voice calls as I climb on to the porch.

"Hey Penelope. I got these for you." I hand her the bouquet of sunflowers. Her eyes light up as she takes them from me.

"Sunflowers! Oh my God, they're so beautiful!" She hugs me quickly and runs toward the kitchen. I let myself in and followed behind her.

"Momma, look what dad got me." I stand still in shock at her calling me dad.

"Pen, I told you that you needed to talk to him before calling him dad. Let's put these in water." She takes the flowers from her.

"Got you some too. Except they are roses." I hand Remmy the rose's and bend down to look Penelope in the eyes.

"I would be honored if you call me dad, Penelope. Thank you," I say, before standing back up.

"Why don't you go outside to play while Bubba and I cook dinner?" Remmy says to Penelope.

"See told you he wouldn't mind," she says, as she runs through the house.

"Don't run in the house!" Remmy yells at her back.

"Are you sure you're ready for this?" She peers up at me.

"Yes. More than ready, Remington." I kiss her on her forehead and take the flowers from her and remove the plastic. I take a knife from the block and cut the ends of the roses as she places two vases on the counter and drops an aspirin and pours water into them. I put the rose's into the vases and set them on the table.

"Thank you Bubba." Remmy steps closer to me and wraps her arms around my neck to kiss me. I pull her up and sit her on the counter to kiss her properly. We are intertwined with hands roaming when my mother walks in.

"Beaufort Allen Williams, you have some explaining to do." She stands holding Penelope's hand and the other on her hip. "This young lady just informed me she came all the way from Ohio to meet her daddy, Bubba. Since you're the only Bubba around here, I am pretty sure she is talking about you. Is there something you have forgotten to tell me?"

"Well shit!" I say, as I step away from Remmy.

"Mom, Dad just said a bad word." Penelope says, as Remmy jumps off the counter her face is as red as a beet.

Looking at the floor she says, "Mrs. William's we were just about to cook supper, would you like to stay and join us?"

"Grandma's staying." Penelope states as she pulls my mother back to the living room.

"It didn't look like y'all was cooking when I walked in." My mother shouts and Remmy looks embarrassed to death, then we both start to laugh.

Chapter Thirty-Eight

Remington

Bubba helped me throw together tacos for supper. After we ate, I sent Penelope up to her room so Bubba and I could tell his mother everything. I was embarrassed to tell her about what my father had done to me, but I managed to get the story out without me crying. On the other hand, she had tears in her eyes the whole time.

"If I had known Remmy, you could have moved in with us." Her hand clasps over mine. "None of us knew Remmy, you poor child. The horror you went through, I can't even imagine."

I hug her and she holds me close and I haven't felt this comforted in a long time. I missed this feeling. The feeling of being genuinely cared about by someone besides Penelope and Gen.

"I am sorry I didn't tell you, Mary, but I was embarrassed and didn't want anyone to know."

"Hush child, nothing to be sorry about. You and that beautiful girl are back home where you belong and you have Bubba and me. We are family." She wipes a tear from her eye and gets up. "I think I'm going to head home. Bubba, you better bring my granddaughter to visit me." She hugs us both before leaving.

"Momma, can we watch a movie?" Penelope says, as she comes out of the room. "I want dad to watch one with us." She uses the puppy dog face, with big sad eyes and aims it at Bubba.

"I can't say no to that," he says, as he sits down on the couch and taps the spot next to him. Penelope crashes beside him and I sit beside her as we flip through movies finally deciding on the Little Rascals.

Penelope's eyes start to drift close, and when she falls asleep on Bubba's lap. I picked her up and put her in Genevieve's bed for the night. I stroll back to the living room, where Bubba is still sitting and I scramble up into his lap. His arms wrap around me and pull me tight. I place my head on his chest.

"You're not leaving me again, Remington. I want you and Penelope to stay. We can sell our houses and get something together. I want you to be my wife and I want to immediately get started on making Penelope a brother or sister." His hand runs through my hair as I gaze up at him.

"Are you sure that's what you want Bubba? If I take her out of school, move back, I want to know that you are all in."

"I was always all in Remington. I would have married you back then, if you would have given me the chance. You're mine and you've always been mine and we need to make it official and I want my name put on Penelope's birth certificate. I want this more than anything I have ever wanted my whole entire life." He kisses me then, with his whole body and soul, and my heart feels so full like it might spill over. I take his hand as I glide off his lap and pull him into my bedroom. I lock the door behind us.

"You're spending the night."

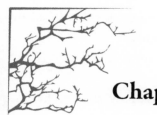

Chapter Thirty-Nine

Bubba

Remmy strips her clothes off as I remove mine and we clash together, hands all over each other. I turn her around so her back is against my chest as my hands roam her body.

"Are you wet for me, Remmy?" I whisper in her ear. As I drop kisses along her neck. She nods her head, but that's not good enough for me.

"I need the words sweetness, talk to me," I growl into her ear.

"Yes," she moans, as I slip my fingers into her wet heat.

"God, I love how wet you get for me," I say, as I fill her up with my fingers, my thumb brushing her clit, causing her to tighten around me. Removing my fingers, she whimpers from the loss. "Bend over the bed baby."

I spit in my hand and rub it all over the length of my cock, Remmy's pussy is glistening with her wetness and it makes my mouth water looking at it. I run the head of my dick through her slit before I impale her with it. A mewl slips from her and I rock into her as I grab her breast and with my free hand I pull her hips into me, our body slapping together.

"Give me all you've got," Remmy says, as she bends over farther into the bed bringing her ass up so I can thrust into her without holding back, and I do. Hard and fast, I kiss her back as I do. With every moan and groan she makes I pound harder, my hand moves from her hip and fists her hair pulling her up into me. Remmy screams my name as she chases her release, I soon follow after and when I come down, I look her in the eyes.

"I love you, Remmy," I say, pulling her to me.

"I love you most," she sighs. "We are going to stay, I will sell this house and we can choose one together as a family."

I kissed her forehead. "You have to marry me first."

"Done. Let's get married at Blue Moon."

"I think that's a wonderful idea, Sweetness." I say, as I pull her into my arms and hold her tight.

It doesn't take long before a light snore comes from my girl. I place her leg over mine and fall asleep with the woman of my dreams in my arms.

A POUNDING ON THE DOOR has me jolt awake, the covers are all askew and wrapped around us.

"Momma, I'm hungry and Auntie Gen didn't come home last night." Penelope yells from the otherside of the door.

I climb out of bed and hurriedly throw my clothes on and open the door. "Come on little miss, let's go see what your mom has to cook for breakfast. Your momma's asleep so we will let her rest for a bit longer."

Her little eyes peer up at me. "Okay, dad. Let's go make momma and us something good." She smiles and my heart feels like it could bust. This is the way the last ten years should have been. My girls are at home with me.

"It looks like we have eggs and bacon and there is bread for toast," Penelope says, as she places a carton of eggs on the counter.

"Can you scramble eggs into the bowl?" I ask, cutting open the bacon package and turning on the stove.

"Yes, I'm ten years old! I help momma and Auntie Gen cook all the time," she says, cracking an egg and emptying it into the bowl.

I place the pan on the stove and put the bacon in. "Crispy or fatty?"

"Duh, crispy," she says, as she mixes up the eggs.

"What are you two doing?" A sleepy eyed Remmy walks into the room and kisses Penelope's cheek.

"Good morning, baby girl." She tussles her hair and then walks up to me and kisses my cheek too.

"I am not a baby." She wipes off her kiss and makes a disgusted face.

"You will always be my baby." She replies and then kisses me again.

"We are making breakfast. You can cook the toast." I say, flipping the bacon.

"I think I can handle that." She giggles, as she opens the bread and puts two pieces in the toaster.

We finished cooking our feast and sat down at the table. "Penelope, what if me and your mom get married soon? Would you like that?"

"Like how soon?" She stuffs a whole piece of bacon in her mouth and chews, "like a year or a month?"

"Don't talk with your mouth full, Pen," Remmy scolds, taking a bite of her eggs.

"Yes ma'am."

"How about next week?" I say, and both women look at me with a shocked face.

"Hell yeah let's get married!" Penelope jumps from her seat and hugs me.

"Pen, you can't cuss either." Remmy says to her daughter before turning to me. "We didn't discuss this."

"Next week sounds good to me." Penelope chimes in, sitting back down.

"I *Guess* it sounds good to me too," Remmy says, as she drinks her coffee, "I need a dress and things."

"You've got a week." I finish off my bacon and give her a smile.

"What's going on?" Genevieve walks into the room and snatches a piece of bacon out of Penelope's plate.

"Hey that's mine," she says, crossing her arms. "Mom and dad are getting married next Saturday, Auntie Gen!"

"Looks like you need a bridesmaid," Gen says, grabbing a slice of toast from Remmy's plate and the rest of her coffee. "I will take time off work. Hurry up and eat. Us ladies have shopping to do! I am going to shower back in twenty minutes."

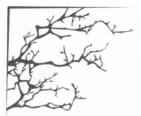

Chapter Forty

Remington

One week later...

"Girl, you look stunning," Arlene says, as she walks into the employee lounge.

"You are sexy as hell." Genevieve replies to Arlene as she checks her out. "Hi, I'm Genevieve, the bestie." She holds her hand out for Arlene to shake.

"Hi, I'm Arlene. Bubba's bestie and ex-fuck buddy. Nice to meet you." Then they both laugh.

"I guess that means you aren't into girls, huh?"

"Not since college." She winks, causing us all to laugh.

"Auntie Gen only dates girls." Penelope pipes in.

"Are you ready?" Samantha comes into the room, her hair a mess and her lipstick smudged.

"Yes. I am, but you need some help. You are a mess." I get up and help fix Samantha's hair and hand her a tissue to fix her smudged lipstick.

The song signaling the bridesmaids start and Penelope, Arlene, Samantha and Genevieve line up and walk out one by one on their que.

When the wedding March begins to play I walk out and down the makeshift aisle to the back of the saloon next to the bullpit to where the love of my life waits.

TWO MONTHS LATER...

"Time for school Penelope!" I call out as she bounces out of her room. "The bus will be here soon."

"Coming momma!" She says, as she gives me a hug. "Are you going to tell dad about the baby?"

"The what?" Bubba walks in and looks at me then at Penelope then back at me.

"I am going to have a baby sister!" Penelope screams and runs to Bubba. "Momma said I could help take care of her."

"We're pregnant?" Bubba looks at me and I shake my head yes, removing the pregnancy test from my pocket. "I was going to tell you."

"Must have been the night on the bull." He gives me a sexy grin and kisses me.

"Come on dad. I've got school." Penelope takes Bubba's hand and drags him towards the front door.

"Okay, little miss. I'm coming." He says before asking. "What if it's a baby brother?"

"I'll love it anyways." Penelope responds and I shake my head.

I never thought that my life would end up like it has. Back in my hometown, back with my first love, with my daughter and with a baby on its way. My heart has never been so full. My life started off in hell, and now I'm in my own slice of heaven and I couldn't ask for more.

The End.

Milton Keynes UK
Ingram Content Group UK Ltd.
UKHW010932231123
433129UK00001B/90